THE EARL OF ZENNOR
THE LEAGUE OF ROGUES
BOOK XVIII

LAUREN SMITH

ISBN: 978-1-960374-26-4 (e-book edition)

ISBN:978-1-960374-27-1 (print edition)

CHAPTER 1

Penzance, England, April 1822

"YOU KNOW WHAT'S WRONG WITH YOU, TRYSTAN?"

Trystan Cartwright, the Earl of Zennor, arched a
dark brow at one of the two men seated across from him
at the table in the grimy little tavern.

Graham Humphrey, a blond-haired gentleman with
gray eyes lit with dangerous mischief, grinned at Trystan.
His companion was Phillip, the Earl of Kent, a solemn
man with a nature so honest he made up for Trystan and
Graham's roguish ways. Graham and Phillip were two of
his most trusted friends, the only ones who could rein
him in when his recklessness began to spiral.

"What?" Trystan asked, his tone laconic as he lifted his glass and downed the scotch within it.

"You're bored. You get testy when you have nothing to do," Graham observed.

"He's not wrong," Phillip added. "And often, what entertains you is not anything I would recommend." He hesitated before continuing in a more careful tone. "What you need is a wife."

Trystan snorted. "No, not yet. Perhaps not ever. Wives can be useful, but they are hardly entertaining. They are shackles that bind men to early graves."

"Wives can open doors that men cannot," Phillip said sagely. "Take a woman with breeding who has been raised to be familiar with the ins and outs of society, women like Audrey St. Laurent or Lady Lennox, who have a knowledge of business and politics. They have a vast amount of power and influence in not just feminine circles."

"But what do I need with power and influence? I have plenty already," Trystan replied. "Besides, you can turn any woman into a society creature. Feed her the right lines, put her in the right clothes and she'd fit like any goose with a gaggle of geese."

"Are you joking? You can't take just anyone and turn them into a lady. Ladies are raised from birth to think and behave a certain way," Graham argued.

"Maybe that's the problem. Perhaps I'd rather

converse with a street urchin than another boring lady of society. They all bore me."

Graham chuckled. "You need a *mistress*, not a wife, obviously," he said, and took a swig of his ale. "Mistresses are amusing, but they require funds to keep them happy. My last mistress cost me a townhouse and half the jewels in London to keep her happy." Graham frowned, as though he hadn't really considered the cost until that moment. That was to be expected. Graham rarely gave anything much thought. He simply did what he wished and damn the consequences. It was why he and Trystan got along famously.

Trystan sighed. "I'm afraid even mistresses bore me." His gaze wandered over the shabby little tavern. Its grubby wallpaper was peeling in places, the tables needed more than a good scrubbing, and the man they'd paid for drinks looked as though he had gone a few rounds in a pugilist match.

Trystan preferred their usual club, Boodle's, but they were far from London and bound for his home in Zennor, which meant reputable places shrank in number the further they strayed from civilization. Zennor, despite its rural location, wasn't all that bad; Trystan could admit that much. His ancestral home was built near the coast of Cornwall, and he liked the way the wind swept in off the sea and how the deep blue water burst into white foam as it careened into the rocky cliffs that banked the sea.

As much as he enjoyed the pleasures of a city like London, he felt an undeniable draw to his home, the many rooms of the rambling manor house full of memories of an adventurous, though sometimes lonely, boyhood. After his mother passed away when he'd been but a boy of ten, he and his father had grown close. He'd learned to appreciate the land and the home that had only a few years ago become his when his father had suffered a stroke and joined his mother.

After his father's death, Trystan had taken to the life of an earl with relative ease. He did not squander his family's fortune on drink, gambling, or other vices. His recklessness came in the form of what entertained him... usually something that would cause Phillip to frown and lecture him on responsibility. His two old school friends were the proverbial angel and devil on his shoulders, offering temptation and temperance in turn, which in its own way was an entertainment.

Trystan swept his gaze over the tavern again, this time taking in the occupants. Everyone here came from a hardscrabble life. Most looked to be dockworkers or sailors. It was possible even a few pirates still sailed into the seaside village.

As aristocrats, Trystan, Graham, and Phillip stood out from the crowd, and because of this they were earning more than a few curious looks from the more brutish men who huddled by the hearth on the opposite side of the room. The speculative looks these men were sending his way could result in trouble, which only made Trystan smile.

Perhaps these men would attack them in hopes of getting some coin. Wouldn't that be a nice change of pace? He could do with a good brawl. He had studied for years at Jackson's Salon with the best boxers in London, and had even managed to give the legendary Earl of Lonsdale a few good swipes.

Graham waved the barkeeper over to bring them more ale. "What you need, my friend, is a challenge."

"I do, but I cannot think of a single thing that could hold my interest." He played with the rim of his cup, gently stroking a fingertip along its smooth edge.

"How about a wager?" Graham said.

Phillip rolled his eyes. "You two and your bloody wagers. Didn't you learn anything the last time when you freed that bear in that dogfighting ring?"

Trystan laughed. "I've never seen so many men run and scream like children when that poor beast got free." he said. "You have to admit we did a good thing, though, Phillip. That bear should never have been held in chains and forced to fight like that."

Phillip closed his eyes and rubbed them with his thumb and index finger. "As much as it pains me to admit it, yes, but the only reason no one was mauled to death was because of that Scottish fellow who was there to calm it down. If he hadn't had such a gift with animals, you both might have been killed, and the beast as well."

Trystan remembered that night all too well—and the surge of power he'd felt at freeing the beast and watching it chase the men who'd tormented it. But Phillip was right, the bear would have eventually killed someone if Aiden Kincade hadn't been there to soothe the creature and trap it in a coach outside the warehouse where the beast had been held captive.

"All's well that ends well. The bear is now in Scotland and we're still here to wager yet again on something ridiculous." He was, however, far from convinced that there was anything new he could bet on that would entertain him for long.

A serving boy brought them more ale, slamming the tankards down hard enough that the ale sloshed out of the cups.

"Ho, there! Watch it, boy!" Trystan snapped at the lad.

"Watch yerself, milord!" the boy countered sharply and stalked back to the bar.

"Impertinent lad," Graham observed. "As I was saying—"

There was a loud crash near the bar. The boy had

tripped and a tray of mugs now lay shattered on the ground.

"Daft fool!" The barman swung a hand and cuffed the boy across the face. The boy crumpled to the floor with a sharp cry of pain.

Trystan, Graham, and Phillip all tensed.

"He was impertinent, but he didn't deserve that," Graham said.

"Do that again and I'll sell you to the whorehouse!" the barman roared. He kicked the boy's ribs as the lad got on his hands and knees to collect the pieces. He fell onto his back and his cap dislodged, sending a tumble of long dark hair down in a messy, oily tangle.

"Bloody hell... It's a girl," Trystan murmured to his friends as they all stared in amazement at the creature on the floor. She was small, dirty cheeked, not the least bit attractive, and had a waspish tongue, but she was still a girl and shouldn't have been hit like that.

"You try to sell me, and I'll cut your bloody heart out and sell it to the bleedin' butcher, you bastard!" the girl shot back at the barman. Despite his best intentions, Trystan found himself smiling at the girl's courage.

"There's a girl with fire in her belly," Graham said. "That's a female who would never be tamed into a quiet, biddable lady of society." he laughed, but Trystan wasn't laughing.

He stared at the girl as she picked up a piece of

broken mug and hurled it back at the barman. The clay shard smashed against the wall next to the man's balding head. Then she ran outside before the bellowing pig could catch her.

For a second the taproom was silent. Then everything went back to normal, laughing and jeering and drinking. The little hellion was gone and no one seemed to care.

"Fancy that. A drink *and* a show," said Graham.

Trystan's lips twitched as he stared at the door the girl had vanished through a moment before.

"Christ, he has that look again," Phillip muttered.

Graham was less concerned and looked hopefully at Trystan. "What is it? What's your idea?" He knew his friend too well.

Trystan leaned back in his chair, a smug smile now spreading across his face as he gripped his mug of ale.

"I wager I can turn that whelp of a girl into a proper lady in one month."

"*That one?* The hellcat who threatened to cut a man's heart out? I just said you couldn't possibly make a girl like that a lady," Graham sniggered. "You might want to be careful she doesn't cut yours out."

"Yes, *that one.*" Trystan smiled wickedly at the thought of such a challenge.

"If you turn her into a proper lady, one to rival a duchess like Emily St. Laurent, I'll pay you two hundred pounds." Graham volunteered the vast sum of money as if it barely mattered.

"Throw in that black-and-red racing curricle and your fastest pair of geldings, and I'll take that bet," Trystan offered.

Graham eyed him thoughtfully. "What if we make it more interesting? Lady Tremaine's ball is in a month. If you bring that girl to the ball and she fools everyone, you win. But if *anyone* sees through her disguise and you fail, you owe me..." Graham drew out his next words in wicked delight. "The deed to your hunting lodge in Scotland. I rather fancy it."

"High stakes indeed, just the way I like it." Trystan chuckled. To have so much to lose only heightened the excitement of the wager, and his friends knew it.

"Now, hold on a minute," Phillip interjected. "This is a *woman*, albeit a rough and ill-mannered one. We must set some rules for propriety's sake."

"Rules?" Graham scoffed at the same moment Trystan replied, "Propriety?"

"Yes," Phillip insisted. "If you both do as you're planning, that woman will be under your control, Trystan. You will be responsible for her. That means you cannot turn her into a mistress or take advantage of her. You must think about her future. What reason does she have to accept your terms, and what will you do once the wager is over? Toss her back into this bar and tell her to carry on as before?"

Trystan laughed. "You honestly think I'd take advantage of *that* creature? Lord, Phillip, I have standards. I thought she was a bloody boy, for Christ's sake. The little hellion has nothing to fear from me. I shall not touch her. Not even if she begs me and not unless I lose my own sanity." He was still chuckling at the thought. He had his pick of women to share his bed, and certainly wouldn't choose a bloodthirsty guttersnipe like the creature he'd just seen.

"Good." Phillip relaxed. "You *both* must deal with this girl with some sense of decorum and chivalry."

Trystan snorted, and Graham only laughed into his mug of ale.

"Enough talking," Graham said. "Get to it, Trystan. Claim the girl, and let's be on our way."

Trystan stood, took his time dusting his waistcoat off, and then he walked over to the barman. He braced his arms on the bar and leaned forward to speak to him.

"Was that hellion whelp yours?" he asked the man.

"Whelp?" The barman seemed confused by the word.

"Yes, the girl you kicked like a starving dog."

The heavyset gray-haired man scratched his chin, eyes narrowing in suspicion at Trystan. "What if she is mine?"

"Then I wish to buy her from you." Trystan expected

the man to show at least a minor concern for the girl's treatment or at least pretend to care what Trystan might do with her, but he didn't so much as ask about Trystan's intentions.

"How much are you willing to pay?"

Trystan stared at the man before he reached for his coin purse and tossed fifty guineas on the table.

"There's fifty," Trystan said.

The man smacked his lips and decided to press his luck. "I could make double off her if I sell her to the whorehouse, plus profits on top of that."

"No madame at a brothel would split any profits with you. She would buy the girl and that would be the end of it. You and I both know it. And she certainly wouldn't pay you fifty guineas for that girl."

"Throw in another five then. She is my stepdaughter, after all, and I love her dearly."

Trystan let out an exasperated sigh. "I'm sure you do, old chap." He slapped another five guineas down beside the rest. Then he returned to his friends at the table and finished his mug of ale.

"How much did she cost you?" Graham asked, trying to hide his devil-may-care grin.

"Fifty-five guineas." He wouldn't miss a single coin, not with the excitement of his wager to look forward to.

Graham whistled. "Expensive girl."

Phillip looked heavenward and cringed. "You two are absolute barbarians."

"Perhaps we are, but what a challenge this will be." Trystan smiled with relish. "I assume you'll come with us to watch over the girl and play her nursemaid?"

His friend gave a weary sigh, but there was a hint of humor in his eyes. "I suppose I had better. Although, I would argue, you two are the ones in need of a nursemaid."

Ignoring Phillip's remark, Trystan looked about the taproom. "Now, to find the little hellcat..." He started for the door and his two friends followed. He was a little more drunk than perhaps he ought to be, but he was quite looking forward to the adventure of turning this hellcat into a fine lady.

❧

BRIDGET RINGGOLD HUDDLED AGAINST THE SIDE OF the tavern, cloaked in shadows while she nursed her wounds. Her stepfather's blow had split her lip, and her ribs ached. She'd be damned lucky if they weren't broken. Her chest would be purple in a few hours after the kick she'd taken. Blood filled her mouth with a foul taste, and it stung each time she ran her tongue over her lip.

She shivered against the brisk fall wind that blew in

off the sea. She wished desperately she could sneak back in the kitchens and warm herself, but the odds of her stepfather finding and striking her again were too high. That meant she would be sleeping in the stables tonight.

Bridget needed to find a way out of this town and into a new life, one that did not involve spending time on her back in a brothel. She was old enough to be on her own—nineteen, in fact—but had few decent options open to her. She could cook a little, could clean a bit, but not well enough to earn a decent living at either. She'd had plenty of men offer her marriage, but none of them were good or decent men. One had almost certainly been a pirate. If only her mother had been here to offer advice, to help her find a way in life either by counsel or helping her find someone to share her life with.

Her mother had died ten years ago, leaving Bridget with a beast of a stepfather. She'd been too young to learn any skills that a woman ought to learn from her mother and had been too busy just trying to survive the dangers of living with a man like her stepfather.

Pushing away from the side of the tavern, she crossed the cobblestone courtyard and ran into the stables. The loft above was quiet and no one ever came up there, aside from the occasional stable boy who forked down hay for the horses. Bridget climbed up the ladder and crawled through the haystacks until she found her nest made of blankets that formed her bed.

She had nicked the blankets here and there over the last year from drunken travelers not minding the belongings in their coach while they went into the tavern for a drink.

She checked for the cloth bag that contained her few treasures, something she did out of habit every night before she settled into sleep. The comb and the mirror had been her mother's, along with several shillings she'd made by whittling wood into the shape of animals.

People passing through Penzance seem to like her figurines. She'd managed to sell or barter three or four of them each week for the last few years, which gave her a little money to afford extra food and clothes as she had grown older. She never wore dresses. Aside from the expense of having gowns made, it was easier and safer to wear clothing meant for men. The locals knew she was a woman, but with a grimy face and hair pinned up beneath a cap, she managed to avoid the interest of most men who passed through the tavern while she served drinks.

Even those fancy gents tonight hadn't known when she'd served their drinks. She'd been watching them too, out of the corner of her eye, and had been rather nervous when her stepfather had ordered her to take more ale to them. But she'd done what she'd always done when she got nervous—she overcompensated with confidence. She couldn't afford to be a fragile flower; she couldn't fake her strength or confidence.

But that had been a mistake. The three men had paid more attention to her because of her impertinence than she'd meant them to. They were a handsome lot, with their finely embroidered waistcoats and polished boots that gleamed in the lamplight. Even the one who'd come in leaning heavily on a cane had been a handsome fellow. Men shouldn't be *that* attractive, Bridget thought with a frown. Especially the one with dark hair and honey-brown eyes. He had an intensity that she didn't like one bit, as if he could read anyone's thoughts simply by meeting their gaze. That one was dangerous.

"But I'm out here, and they're in there," she murmured to herself. No one ever disturbed her up in the loft, because no one thought to look in the haystacks.

She busied herself by inventorying the rest of her possessions, which included a small carving knife that was tucked away in the back of the bag. Once she was assured her treasures were safe, she settled down to sleep and tugged her blankets up over her. She heard the horses below, nickering softly as they ate oats and hay. The scuttling of mice somewhere on the rafters, rather than frightening her, assured her she was safe. Mice always moved about when no one else was around.

She had closed her eyes and started to drift when the

scurrying mice stopped and the stables turned quiet. A moment later, low voices whispered to each other from below.

"She must be in here. I saw her cross the courtyard as we came out," a man said. His cultured voice was one she recognized, belonging to one of the fancy gents. His voice was smooth as warm brandy, and she remembered his eyes were the same color. Bridget slid free of her blankets and moved silently along the floor of the loft so she could peer over the edge. Three men stood in the center of the stables, looking around.

Bridget ducked down as far as she could to avoid being seen by them.

"Trystan, no one's here," one of the other men said.

"She's here," the first man said with a soft chuckle. "Aren't you, little hellcat? Come out, child! I bought you from that wretch who claims to be your stepfather, and I'm here to discuss your future."

"Trys, you'll scare her. Tell the girl what you plan to do for her first, or she'll think you mean her harm," one of the men argued.

The loft vibrated as the man began to climb up the stairs of the ladder. Bridget would have shoved the ladder away and sent the man crashing to the floor, but that would leave her no easy way to escape. If she tried to make that drop, she would most likely break an ankle or her neck, and she was injured enough as it was.

Thinking quickly, she dug through her bag until she found her whittling knife. It was a small blade, but it could still cut them if they tried anything. But her best chance was to not be seen at all.

The man reached the top of the loft, searching the dim, hay-strewn platform. It was just dark enough inside the stables that he might miss her.

Please don't let him see me, please.

She held her breath, and the blood roared so loud in her ears she couldn't hear much else.

"Gotcha!" With his feet still planted on the top rung of the ladder, the man lunged for her. Bridget scrambled back, but one of his hands gripped her ankle and dragged her toward him. She kicked at him with her foot and caught his chin. He grunted in pain but didn't let go. Instead, her fight seemed to light a new fire in him. He climbed fully into the loft and dove at her. Bridget raised the knife just as he landed on top of her, and she felt the blade scrape across his arm.

"Christ, she has a knife!" The man bellowed as he pinned her flat on the floor.

He grasped her wrist, stopping the hand holding the knife, and pressed it hard against the floor beside her head.

"Let go of it, hellion!"

"No!" she spat.

"Let go!" His grip tightened to the point of pain,

forcing her to drop the knife. His grip instantly eased and the pain vanished.

"Er... I say, Trystan. Let's be quick about this," one of the man's friends said. "It looks as though we're kidnapping this girl, when that's not really the case. I don't wish to be here long, lest we find ourselves in trouble. Our coach is ready."

Trystan stared down at her, the hard angles of his face too perfect for any man, especially one as wicked as the devil himself.

"Listen, little cat," he growled. "I bought you tonight from that swine who claims to be your stepfather. I have no plans at all to hurt you, except to spank that ass of yours if you dare to stab me again."

"I ain't no whore!" Bridget spat angrily. "Don't you dare touch me!"

"Of that, I'm very aware," he replied. "And that's not why I bought you. Come down with me, and my friends and I will explain just what I plan to do with you."

Bridget didn't want to go anywhere with a man she didn't know, let alone *three*.

"Go to hell," she snapped, but she was all too aware that he was fully on top of her and could do anything he wished to her if he wanted. His weight didn't crush her, but she was fully pressed into the floor by his body, trapped and helpless. Something wild fluttered in her lower belly that made her feel strange.

THE EARL OF ZENNOR

"Graham, find some rope, please. The little cat refuses to withdraw her claws," Trystan shouted over his shoulder to one of the two men waiting below.

"Miss..." the third man's voice gently called out. "We really mean you no harm."

Bridget spat, "You're trying to bloody nab me. Ain't nothing innocent about that." Her protest was silenced as Trystan rolled his eyes and shoved a wadded handker- chief into her mouth.

"There, that's better." He grasped both of her wrists in one hand and dragged her toward the ladder. She fought valiantly, and he soon seemed to realize he could not force her down the ladder. He peered over the side of the loft and then before she could stop him, he scooped her up and tossed her.

She screeched and a second later landed in a wagon of hay just below. Trystan climbed down the ladder and pulled her from the hay.

"Rope, Graham." Trystan held out his hand.

The one not leaning on a cane passed Trystan a coil of rope, which her captor used to bind her wrists tightly together. Then he held her still, with one strong hand gripping her arm. She was trussed up like a sheep for slaughter.

"We need to get her into the coach. I don't want that barman changing his mind. She's got too much spirit to end up in a brothel," Trystan announced.

Confused by his words, she stumbled along as Trystan pushed her to follow his two companions into the waiting coach. She panicked, trying to spit out the gag. Her bag, her things... all that she had in the world was still in the stables. Tears streamed down her face, and one of the men noticed.

"We aren't going to hurt you," said the one who used his cane to walk about. His eyes were gentle as he looked upon her. "Please don't cry, Miss. Everything will be all right. Now please, don't scream. I give you my word no one will hurt you." He removed the handkerchief from her mouth just as the other two men sat down. The dark-haired devil named Trystan chose the seat directly beside her, and she was suddenly warmed by the heat of his body.

"Please—please, milord. My bag... I ain't got nothing else."

Trystan lifted up her cloth bag. "You mean this?"

She sighed in relief. "Yes, that's the one."

"I'm tempted to search it for weapons," he mused as he started to open the mouth of it.

"Trystan, really. Give the girl some peace, will you?" the kind one said. Then he turned her. "My name is Phillip Wilkes. I'm the Earl of Kent."

"An earl...?" Bridget said, relaxing a little. On the one hand, it seemed inconceivable that a man of high birth would mean her any harm. Then again, it also meant if they did, there was nothing anyone could do to stop them.

"That's right. The man beside you is Trystan Cartwright, the Earl of Zennor."

"Two earls? They just handing out titles to anyone these days?"

Kent smirked and nodded at the third man. "And that is Graham Humphrey."

"Not as fancy as your friends. No title to wave about?" she taunted. Graham's gray eyes narrowed on her.

"Some of us don't *need* a title to wave about. Some of us are wicked enough without it," Graham warned her. But something about him didn't scare her like it should have. He seemed like a man who would tease a woman and make her laugh, rather than threaten her.

Trystan burst out laughing. "Lord, what fun this will be!"

"Fun? What do you plan to do with me?" Bridget demanded. "I'll not share your bed if that's—"

"Heavens, no! On that we agree," Trystan tutted before he dramatically shuddered. "No, no, my little hellcat. Graham and I have made a wager, about *you*."

Bridget didn't like the sound of that. Wagers were made by either bored men or desperate ones, and she didn't want to be involved with either.

"I have one month to turn you into a proper lady, Miss... Lord, I don't even know your name."

"It's Bridget. Bridget Ringgold. And wot do you mean a proper *lady?*" Bridget echoed, drawing out the word. "Why would you want to do that?"

"Because I am bored," Trystan supplied.

A bored gentleman. It was as she had feared.

"I ain't no doll to dress up and play with," she argued.

"It's 'am not,' and yes, you are my doll, girl. I *bought* you. For the next month, I will dress you and teach you to do things that I want you to do. In one month's time, you will walk, talk and look the part of a duchess, by God. By the end of all this, you will likely be able to catch some man in a parson's mousetrap, and you will have a far better life than the one you currently have. You will be singing my praises instead of trying to turn me into a pincushion."

She plum forgot she had pricked him with her blade, but he didn't seem to be hurting.

"You ain't hurt none, milord. If you was, you'd be bleeding all over the blooming place," she pointed out sourly, secretly wishing she'd had better aim and had stabbed his heart.

"I *am* hurt, but I'll deal with it later." He nodded toward his sleeve, and she realized that she'd cut through his coat and down to his flesh. Even in the dim light of the coach, she could see he was bleeding now. If he was hurting, what sort of man could hide a pain like that? Bridget fell into a worried silence.

"Trystan is right," Kent said. "In a month's time, you will have a whole new set of skills. I expect you will be able to find a man to propose to you who can offer you a fine life with fancy gowns, a coach at your disposable, and a life without worries. Wouldn't that be lovely?"

She shot Kent a sour look. "An' who says I need a man?" she fired back.

Graham was the one who laughed this time. "Christ, you're right, Trystan. This is going to be fun."

Fun for them, perhaps, but Bridget wanted no part of this silly wager. She'd take advantage of a roof over her head and food while she planned her next move. Perhaps she'd nick a bit of that fine silverware the toff no doubt possessed and start a new life with the money that silver would fetch her. Then *she* would be the one laughing.

CHAPTER 2

Bridget bided her time, although that proved difficult. She never was good at being patient. It was one of her numerous failings, and she was all too aware of that as she fought her natural urge to fidget. They traveled another three hours and just as dawn crested the horizon, their carriage made a stop at a coaching inn to allow the horses time to rest.

"Tell me we're staying a while, Trys." Graham grumbled like a weary child.

"We could push on," Trystan suggested.

Much to Bridget's amazement, he seemed unaffected by his lack of sleep, while Bridget, Graham, and Kent were all fighting to stay awake.

"We could." Kent stuffed a fist against his mouth as he fought off a yawn. "But honestly, I am exhausted. We haven't slept since we left London. Staying here for a few hours won't hurt us."

Bridget yawned as Kent had. "I could go for a bit of shuteye too, milord. Been working all day and night serving gents like you and getting nothing but my ears boxed for it. I ain't had no proper rest in ages."

"I agree, let the girl rest," Kent said diplomatically. "We could travel again around noon. It would give us six hours or so to recover." Kent was by far her favorite of the three men. She'd decided to think of him by his title, because he was a true gentleman, unlike the other two toffs who made her spitting mad.

Outnumbered, Trystan let out an aggrieved sigh. "Very well."

He leapt out of the coach and spoke to the driver. Graham followed him. Kent shared a sleepy smile with Bridget, then climbed out and turned to offer her his hand. Bridget stared at her bound wrists as she got to her feet and stood at the opening of the coach.

"Careful, my dear. Allow me," Kent said. He changed his mind about taking her hand and instead gently grasped her waist and eased her down to the ground.

"Thank you, milord," Bridget said, feeling strangely bashful. She'd seen gentleman help ladies before, but she'd never been one of those ladies. For a moment, Kent had treated her like she was, and there was something rather mystifying and pleasing about that.

In the pale morning light, she saw Graham trudge wearily toward the door of the coaching inn. Trystan handed their coach driver a few coins and then clapped the man on the back with a gloved hand before turning their way.

"Let's go inside, Miss Bridget. Are you hungry? I could have some food brought to break your fast," Kent suggested.

"I'm near starved to death. A bit of vittles would do wonders." In truth, her stomach had been grumbling something fierce for the last several hours.

Kent winked at her. "Then a bit of vittles it is."

Despite her distrust of these three aristocrats, she had to admit that Lord Kent was gracious enough to treat her kindly and not like a piece of property, unlike Trystan. She shot a glare at her darkly handsome tormentor, who followed behind them.

When they stepped inside the common room of the inn, they found it empty except for a few bleary-eyed travelers.

"I'll secure our rooms," Trystan told Kent. "You stay with her."

Kent led Bridget to a table and waved a maid over to place an order.

"Please bring us four servings of whatever you have." Ken slipped a number of coins into the maid's palm. The young woman's eyes widened, and she rushed away with a happy grin.

Bridget raised her bound hands and dropped them dramatically on the table with a thud, then met Kent's startled gaze.

"Will you untie me, milord? Or do you intend to feed me with a spoon?"

Kent considered her request, then reached across the table. With deft fingers, he undid the knots and freed her hands. Bridget rubbed her wrists and gave Kent a thunderous look as he collected the rope and coiled it up before setting it on the table between them.

"I assure you, this is all just for some harmless wager. In a month, you shall have a fine wardrobe and a small dowry to offer any man who might fancy to marry you, or you can go and live your own life. It must be better than the position you had at that wretched tavern."

He wasn't wrong, but Bridget had always hated the idea that a woman's place in the world was defined by the men around her.

"It may have been wretched, milord, but it was *my* wretched. Now you've gone and taken me away from me home, kidnapping me like you did."

Kent chuckled wryly. "Trystan is not a man to do things properly or even logically."

"He's a toff, just like you are. Rich men like him are

used to getting their way, an' don't like takin' no for an answer."

Kent conceded the point. "True. But he's a good man, I assure you. You will only benefit from his lessons on how to be a proper lady."

She snorted ungracefully, and Kent's eyes twinkled with amusement. The maid returned with two plates laden with roast beef, eggs, and a questionable fish-based dish. Bridget helped herself to the meat and eggs as well as the bread, leaving Kent to fend for himself with the plate of fish. He ate it without complaint, but when Graham and Trystan joined them, he was quick to offer them some of his remaining meal.

Graham poked at the fish with a fork. "What's this? Kippers?"

"I'm not quite sure. It's edible," Kent said. "But not that appetizing."

Bridget continued enjoying her own food, but her chewing slowed when she realized Trystan was watching her with a calculated gleam in his eyes that she didn't care for one bit.

"Slow down, Bridget. No one is going to take your food away from you. You're eating like a wild animal."

Her cheeks were puffed out with food. She was used to getting only scraps of whatever was left after the customers were asleep for the night, which was never enough. Food, at least decent food that she could afford, was always scarce. Even the old hound that hung out behind the inn sometimes ate better than she did. Trystan scooted closer to her at the table and reached for the fork she held in her fist, gently prying it from her hand. She swallowed the food in her mouth so she no longer resembled a chipmunk.

"Do you know how to read?" he asked.

"Course I do," she snapped proudly.

"Excellent. There's some intelligence in you, after all." He held out her fork to show her. "Do you see how I'm holding it? Pretend you are going to write. I pray I'm not too presumptuous to assume you can write as well?"

She nodded. "My mom taught me my letters when I was little, but after she died I ain't had no time to practice."

"I see..." Trystan sighed softly. "That at least tells me where your challenges will lie."

"I'll have you know I can read an' write better than half of Penzance," she shot back. "My mother raised me right an' as best she could, God rest her soul." She'd never needed to eat properly or speak properly before, yet here she was with these gents showing her that she was doing not just one thing but *many* things wrong.

"I'm sure she did," Kent agreed in the soothing tone. "But it's easy to learn."

Bridget doubted that. She'd grown up most of her life speaking, acting and eating a certain way. If these men thought she could completely change herself in less than a month, they were fools.

"Let's try eating the *correct* way." Trystan's large hands placed the fork in her fingers and adjusted her grip. Feeling humiliated, Bridget attempted to hold the fork the way he'd shown her. Thankfully, he turned his focus back on his companions, leaving her briefly to puzzle over this new way to eat.

"Have you thought of the story you'll spin when we take this girl to Lady Tremaine's ball? We'll have to explain her presence in some way," Graham said as he pulled one of the plates of food toward himself.

Trystan sliced a bit of his roast beef and took a bite. "I've been thinking about that."

Bridget did her best to imitate him, watching carefully how he used his utensils. He did it with a gentlemanly flair that looked easy, but her fingers felt awkward trying to hold the fork and knife the way he did.

"My great aunt, Lady Helena, will be an excellent chaperone. She lives nearby my estate at the dowager cottage."

Graham snickered like a little boy. "Not that old woman who is half-deaf and carries around that absurd ear trumpet?"

"Yes, *that* aunt." Trystan ignored Graham's glee. "I have a distant cousin in Yorkshire who's quite a bit older than me and avoids society like the plague. I'll say this child is his daughter and that I've agreed to introduce her to society for the season."

"That should work," Kent agreed. "We'll have to make sure Bridget knows your family tree well enough to maintain whatever story you concoct."

Bridget tried to listen while she continued to practice holding the fork the way Trystan showed her. It felt awkward and far less effective in getting the food from her plate to where it belonged—in her mouth. Frustrated, she finally dropped the fork with a clatter on the plate and crossed her arms over her chest, scowling.

"Finished already?" Graham said. She stuck her tongue out at him.

"Do that again, and I will put you over my knee. Act like a child, and I shall treat you like one," Trystan warned, his whiskey-colored eyes blazing.

Bridget swallowed and ducked her head. It was better to play meek around that one, or else he might do exactly what he promised. Bridget's belly was still mostly empty when the men stood up. Their own plates were cleaned of food, but a few pieces of bread had been left behind. She reached out and snatched the bread and shoved it in the pockets of her shabby coat when the three men weren't paying attention.

"Time to sleep." Graham stretched and left the others without a word for his room.

Kent lingered behind. "How many rooms did you—?"

"One for you and Graham, and one for me and the whelp to share."

"Trystan..." Kent protested.

"She'll run the second she has a chance. Won't you, little cat?" Trystan asked.

Bridget, unprepared for the man to guess her secret plans so easily, wasn't able to hide her reaction. She froze, eyes wide when Trystan tried to take her arm.

"Hah, see? The little cat had every intention of escaping, didn't you, pet?" Trystan's dark chuckle made Bridget narrow her eyes.

"I ain't your pet," she hissed. "Call me that again and—"

"And what?" Trystan towered over her, his dark hair falling over his brow. She had the sudden urge to brush it away with her fingers. Startled and more than disturbed by that passing urge, Bridget stepped back. Being so close to him made her stomach tumble. She almost felt queasy, but not in the usual way. She gulped and looked away, breaking the eye contact. She'd let him win this little battle, but she was determined to win the war.

"You're sure you can take care of her?" Kent asked. "And by that, I mean be polite to her?"

Trystan and Kent stared at each other a long moment. "I will treat her as well as she treats me. If she acts polite, I shall be polite."

Kent's shoulders sagged. "Just don't kill each other, that's all I'm asking."

Trystan shot him a devil-may-care grin. "I promise we'll both survive the night. We'll see you back down here at midday." Trystan nodded to Kent as he firmly grasped Bridget's arm and dragged her upstairs.

She was pushed unceremoniously into an empty room with two small beds. Without a word, Trystan removed his coat and dropped it over a chair, then rolled up his sleeves. He grabbed the end of his bed by its wooden headboard and hauled it across the room until it blocked the door from being opened.

Bleedin' hell... The man thought of everything, didn't he?

"There," he muttered with satisfaction as he studied the barred door. Then he started to unbutton his waistcoat and let it drop off his shoulders. Stunned, Bridget half-crouched behind her small bed, watching him. She had seen a few half-undressed men in her day, mostly drunks being dragged out of her stepfather's tavern. But none of them were built like this one. He had a body carved of marble and seeing him bare his flesh was different somehow than seeing those other men. That fluttering in her belly grew stronger, and she flattened a palm on her abdomen, trying to soothe away the strange sensations.

Trystan pulled his shirt over his head and stood there, the cloth draped loosely over his arm, the olive skin of his chest showing off the hard plane of muscles that made Bridget a little dizzy to look at. He was positively indecent, standing there half-naked. A thin red slash marred the skin on his left arm, and a little blood had smeared where the fabric of the shirt had rubbed the wound.

"See something that interests you?" he asked with a dark chuckle.

"Not. At. All." She pronounced each word with clear disgust.

Trystan chuckled. "Your nose wrinkles when you lie," he observed.

He tossed his shirt over the single chair in the room and sat down on his bed to remove his boots. When he was done, he crossed the room to the washstand where a porcelain bowl and a pitcher of water stood in front of a small mirror. He washed the blood off his arm and studied the scratch in the mirror.

"I pricked you good, didn't I?" she said with a bit of pride.

"*Pricked* being the key word," he agreed. "Thank heavens you have no cutthroat talents to worry about. I don't think it will bleed much more now." He said this more to himself than to her. "Get into your bed, hellcat, and sleep well. You'll need it. Once we reach Zennor, you will begin a vigorous training in all aspects of being a fine born woman. The quicker you learn, the more you can

LAUREN SMITH

rest, but fail to learn and it will be that much harder for you."

"Why are you doing this?" she dared to ask.

"Because I refuse to lose my bet to Graham. I rather like my hunting lodge in Scotland, and I should hate to lose it to him simply because you refuse to eat, speak and act like a lady."

Bridget didn't doubt that this man would run her ragged if she wasn't careful. He seemed like a man possessed of more energy than most.

She peeled the bed covers back and climbed in, still fully clothed. She wasn't about to give the man a chance to take advantage of her. She shut her eyes, listening to his bed creak as he lay back and let out a slow breath. Bridget weighed her chances of escaping out the window against him catching her. Somewhere between the planning of her first escape plan and her tenth, she drifted off.

❧

TRYSTAN WAITED UNTIL HE HEARD THE GIRL'S breathing even out, then finally allowed himself to relax. He was certain she would have tried escaping, but he suspected she'd got very little sleep while living and working at that tavern, just as she had gotten very little food. She wasn't malnourished, but she certainly had not been getting enough to eat. That had been evident earlier, when she'd been shoveling down food at a pace he hadn't thought humanly possible. She'd even squirreled away a few bits of bread in her coat pockets for later.

He would make a lady of her. And while the training would be rigorous, he would treat her far better than she'd been treated at the tavern in Penzance. Once they arrived at his home in Zennor, he would have her bathed and scrubbed clean and her measurements taken for the dressmaker, then he would fully assess the challenges he was facing. He lay awake a while longer, planning and plotting how best to win the wager. He couldn't let Graham take his favorite hunting lodge.

Trystan didn't feel all that tired, not like the others. He was possessed with energy from the passion this new enterprise gave him. He couldn't wait to see the faces of the men and women at Lady Tremaine's ball when he presented Bridget to them. His little hellcat would be transformed into a gentle English rose, a demure creature in the most exquisite clothes, and her voice would be a sultry caress upon every man's ear. Gentlemen would come to blows fighting for a spot on her dance card. The women would either be green with envy or desperate to become her friend. She would be a true *original*, and London society simply adored originals. Trystan would have a secret laugh at fooling all of

London by training a wild hellcat into acting the part of a lady.

A smile curved Trystan's lips as he imagined his triumph at the ball. Graham knew better than to make a wager against him like this. While he was a master of trouble and a reckless rogue, he was also well trained in etiquette and all that went with being a titled lord, more so than Graham. As a firstborn son, he'd received the training of the heir of an estate, whereas Graham, as the spare in his family, had less oversight from his parents in such matters.

Trystan slept four hours and then woke fully rested. He was careful not to make any sounds as he got dressed. The girl was still asleep, and he rather liked how quiet it was when she wasn't shouting at him or pricking him with that little blade of hers.

Tempted by the realization that he could get a better look at her while she slept, he tiptoed over to her bed. He braced one hand on the headboard so he could peer down at her. Smudges of dirt covered her face, and her oily hair was tucked up in a mess of pins beneath the cap which had fallen from her head as she slept. He rolled his eyes. She hadn't even washed up before bed.

But something about her face intrigued him. She wasn't beautiful, no, but she was interesting. With a pert chin, heart-shaped face and tilted eyes with long dark lashes, she had a mixture of features that were pleasing.

Her lips were not too plump, nor too thin. Her face had character. A man could look at her and be fascinated all day watching how her expressions would change.

Some women had very little expression. They sat primly with blank, demure looks that did not move Trystan to passion or even casual interest. Such women were completely uninteresting to him. And women *ought* to be interesting. They were the fairer sex; their allure and mystery were supposed to be irresistible to men. And yet far too many were little more than pretty statues to him.

The few women he admired were unafraid to engage in political, economic, or even philosophical discourse. But most women held their tongues and played the part that society expected of them, which always left Trystan deeply disappointed and bored.

Whenever he took a mistress, he gave her his conversation, his time, his interest, his engagement, not simply his body in her bed—although the latter seemed to be what most of them were interested in.

The little hellcat shifted in her sleep, and then her eyelids suddenly fluttered open. The sleepy, delightful drowsiness vanishing as she realized he was towering over her while she lay in her bed. She swung her fist and walloped him soundly in the eye.

"Bloody hell, woman!" he roared as he fell back a step and clutched his eye. Pain radiated from his eye socket down to his cheekbone. It was definitely going to bruise, and Graham was going to crow about it for the next few days.

"What were you doing leaning over me like that, you big galoot?"

"Galoot?" He repeated the word with disbelief. The mouth on this little creature—and her colorful vocabulary—were going to have to be corrected.

"You deserved that, you did. Leanin' over a woman like that." She sat up, fists still raised.

Trystan cursed under his breath and turned to the washstand. His eye was red and his face was starting to swell around it. Graham would never let him live this down. Kent would be more understanding, but he'd no doubt chuckle over this a little too much.

"It was *your* fault," Bridget went on. He clenched his fists and closed his eyes, only to wince at the pain.

"Use the chamber pot if you need to and come to the taproom downstairs when you are ready to leave," he said, instead of all the colorful expressions just waiting to be fired back at the little hellion. He moved the bed out of the way and left the room so she could see to her needs alone.

He found Kent and Graham already awake and eating a bit of lunch.

"Where's the chit?" Graham asked. "Did you lose her already?"

"No, of course not."

"Trystan..." Kent began. "Is your eye...?"

"The hellcat hit me," he said in a tone that did not welcome follow-up questions.

Graham, who had been drinking a mug of ale, spewed it over the table as he choked on laughter. Kent looked more concerned than amused.

"Is there... er... a *reason* that she struck you? You weren't doing anything untoward, were you?" Kent dared to ask.

Trystan arched a brow. "I was merely trying to get a better look at the scamp. She's half dirt beneath those clothes of hers. I thought she was sleeping peacefully, so I wanted to get a closer look at her, but she woke up and saw me leaning over her and *wham!*" He slapped the table with his palm and Graham scrambled to catch his mug before it toppled over.

"And where is she now?" Kent asked.

"Using the chamber pot, and then I suspect she'll try to climb out the window." He reached across the table, stole the fresh apple off Graham's plate and took a bite before he stood and walked to the door of the coaching inn. As he stepped outside, he lingered beneath the eaves of the slanted roof. His room was just above where he stood. Kent and Graham joined him as he waited patiently.

"Maybe she—" Graham began, but Trystan raised a hand, silencing him.

A moment later, the roof creaked above them and then a pair of legs appeared over the edge followed by the body of the little hellcat as she hung off the roof's edge, then dropped to the ground with more grace than Trystan had expected.

"Ahh, Bridget, there you are. Excellent." Trystan stepped out from the shadows and grasped her arm before she could bolt. "How thoughtful of you to join us just in time to board the coach."

"Bleedin' hell!" She shrieked and tried to pull herself free.

Trystan gave her bottom two light swats with his palm, which made her jerk and glare at him, but he saw a heat of another kind in her eyes. The little cat might not know it herself, but she liked getting love pats to the bottom. He was surprised by that she would keep him guessing, this one, and that made this whole adventure worthwhile.

"Kent, please fetch provisions that we can eat on the road." He then escorted Bridget to the waiting coach and pushed her inside. His left eye was swelling shut, and he decided he would spend the remaining journey to his estate planning Bridget's punishment in the form of her first lessons of being a lady. The thought brought a wicked smile to his lips.

CHAPTER 3

So this is Zennor, is it?

Bridget stood in front of the steps of a fine house, bigger than any she'd ever seen. It was built of craggy gray stones that made the medieval manor feel a bit like a castle.

She had never been to Zennor even though it was less than seven miles from Penzance, the town where she had spent her entire life. On the way here, she had traveled through a beautiful, yet desolate countryside and she had found herself falling in love with the rolling hills and jutting cliffs she'd seen. Now she was rather fascinated by Trystan's home as well.

She could do without the owner of course, but his home? She could spend the rest of her life exploring the rambling manor house. She didn't allow herself to be fascinated with the house's owner. She'd been essentially kidnapped by this man and his friends, and they promised they'd treat her right, but she wasn't free to leave. Yet she was admittedly charmed by this place and was tempted to stay, to see what it was like living in a grand house like this.

The ride here had been mostly silent for her. The men had talked with one another, using grand words and speaking of places she didn't know. Even when the Lord Kent had attempted to engage her, she'd held her chin away from them and looked out the window, determined to have her fill of the countryside as it rolled by. She didn't want them to think she was enjoying this journey so far from the only real place she'd called home.

She'd also been distracted by the heat radiating off Trystan, which had warmed her cold body and left her more than aware that even in her silence, the man was watching her, studying her as if he was thinking of all the things he'd do to turn her into a lady. The fancy-pants was fooling himself though. Still, she was tempted to try to play the part of lady if it meant living in this house for a while.

"Well, ain't she a beauty?" she sighed as she looked up dreamily at the front of the house.

"She is, *isn't* she," Trystan said, his voice softening as he stood beside her. "The original house was medieval, of course. You would never know it, given the many improvements made through the generations."

"You don't say? Medieval, is it?" Bridget smirked at his haughty tone.

He spared her a sidelong glance she couldn't interpret. "You *will* find it more than adequate. It has been thoroughly modernized, full of all the creature comforts one could possibly desire."

Bridget didn't know why a posh lord would require *comfortable* creatures, whatever those were, but it was clearly something he was proud of. She'd known very little comfort in her life, except perhaps the warmth of the hay in the stables. Still, she felt the ancient pull of this place deep in her bones. Perhaps it was the way fine chestnut trees lined the path to the house like a forested arrow, or the way the sunset glinted off its many windowpanes. All of it was surrounded by the roar of the sea somewhere beyond the house, which made it feel somehow endless. Like it was a place at the edge of the world, or perhaps at the *beginning* of it.

She had a sudden flash of an old memory of her mother sitting across from her on the floor of a bedchamber with a book of maps laid out between them. Her mother had traced the shape of the ocean at the edge of the map.

"Some people used to believe the world was flat.

When they reached a certain point on the map, they would simply drop off into an abyss."

"Why?" young Bridget had asked.

"Because some people cannot believe in things they do not see. They cannot see beyond the edges of a map, so therefore it must end there. Anything else would be beyond their imaginings. But..." Her mother smiled secretively. "*Some* people can see past the edge of the map and go all the way around the world and then, when they come back to the place they started, they have learned about themselves and the world."

"Did they learn everything about the world?" Bridget asked.

"No," her mother laughed. "No one can know everything. There will always be plenty left to discover, and that is the gift we have living on this earth. We have the ability to endlessly explore and learn, and allow us to grow into better people."

The memory faded, and a fierce heartache overtook Bridget. She placed a palm against her chest. She would've given up all the mysteries of the world just to have her mother by her side again.

A man stepped out of the front door and came down the steps to greet them. "My lord." He was a tall, lean man in his early fifties, but held an air of strength and grace as he moved.

"Ah, Mr. Chavenage," Trystan replied. "Please

prepare two guest rooms for Graham and Philip and one room for Miss Ringgold." Trystan's lips curved in a crooked grin as he glanced between her and Mr. Chavenage. If the man was shocked by Trystan's orders, he didn't show it.

"Yes, my lord. And Miss Ringgold is..." The man eyed her speculatively.

Trystan crossed his arms, gave her a thoughtful, assessing type of look, creating a burn deep within her. Bridget glared at him.

"A project. Please tell Mrs. Story to meet me in my study for instructions about the girl's care."

The man nodded and went back into the house while two strapping young men in footmen's livery came down to the coach and began removing travel cases from the back.

"Who was that?" Bridget asked Lord Kent in a quiet voice as Trystan and Graham proceeded into the house.

"Who?"

"That chap, Mr. Chavenage."

"Oh," Kent chuckled. "That is Trystan's butler. He runs a most efficient house, a good man."

"And this Story lady?"

"Mrs. Story is the housekeeper. They are both fair and kind so long as you treat them the same."

Kent was gently giving her advice as to her behavior.

Bridget made a note not to cross Mr. Chavenage, or Mrs. Story.

"Shall we?" Kent offered her his arm. She stared at it. "Loop your arm through mine and rest your hand here." Kent gently placed her hand the way he wished her to. She'd seen this done before of course, but she'd never done it herself with a man.

While she was perfectly fine to walk without aid, there was something nice about holding onto Kent's arm. He braced himself on his cane as they climbed up the steps. The inside of the house was beautiful, more beautiful than anything she'd ever seen in Penzance. Dark wood paneling covered the lower half of the rooms and was accented by silk wallpapers in various colors, changing from room to room. Gilded sconces lined the walls. Portraits, dozens of them, filled the corridors and trailed up the large staircase.

"Who are they now?" she asked as she studied the fine lords and ladies upon the walls.

"Two or perhaps three centuries' worth of Cartwrights. Trystan's family."

She scrutinized the features painted in layers of oil as she hunted for Trystan's dark hair, whiskey eyes and olive skin, but didn't find them.

"He sure don't look like any of 'em," she said.

"No, I don't," Trystan said as he exited a room at the end of the corridor. "My mother was a Romani woman who the locals say bewitched my father into marriage. Thankfully, it was a happy one." He smiled as he said this, and it softened his face in a way that tugged at her heart.

"Your mum was a gypsy?"

Trystan's eyes hardened slightly. "Yes." His reply was curt. "Now, come here if you please."

"I *don't* please." Bridget clung tight to Kent's arm even though he escorted her straight to Trystan.

"This is my study." Trystan nodded at the room she'd been shown into. "Sit down." He took her by the shoulders, steered her toward a large leather armchair and pushed her onto it. "And *stay*," he added firmly.

A caustic retort died on her lips as she noticed a tall, slightly plump woman staring at her. She wore a dark gray cloth gown and stood next to the large ornate desk inside the study.

"Bridget, this is Mrs. Pearl Story, my housekeeper. You will call her Mrs. Story unless she tells you otherwise. Mrs. Story, this is my little hellcat, Bridget Ringgold."

The housekeeper stared at her. "This is the one ye want me to clean up, my lord?" Her voice had a Scottish accent that Bridget wasn't used to hearing.

Bridget bristled.

"Yes, clean her up and find a spare dress from one of the maids. We'll have a dressmaker brought to the house tomorrow to measure her for a decent wardrobe. Until then, whatever you can find that fits her will do. And burn the clothes she's wearing. I never wish to see them again or smell them."

"Oi! You can't take my clothes and *burn* them!" she cried out. "They're all I got."

"Hush your shrieking!" Trystan barked. "Mrs. Story will dress you in *new* clothes, something that will suit you better than these *rags*." He waved a hand at her soiled garments.

Those *rags* had cost her two months of animal carvings as well as her tavern wages.

"I bought them. They're mine!" she snarled. "You can't take what I work so hard for and—!"

"Easy, girl." Mrs. Story's Scottish accent thickened slightly. "No one will burn anything." The housekeeper shot Trystan an exasperated look, then turned back to Bridget. "We'll clean them up, mend any tears, and give them back to ye."

Trystan and Bridget glared at one another in a silent but heated battle of wills.

"Now, listen here, Bridget. You are to go with Mrs. Story and do whatever she says. If you give her any trouble, you'll deal with me." His tone brooked no argument.

"Come along, Miss Ringgold," Mrs. Story said in a gentle tone. "Let's wash ye up a bit before dinner."

Bridget followed the housekeeper, eyes wide as she

continued to take in the expansive house. She was truly going to stay here?

"I'll show ye where yer room is. His lordship usually has a bath first thing when he arrives, but we've been putting the hot water in yer chambers instead at his request."

She followed the housekeeper up the stairs and down another hall until the woman paused and opened the door. A pair of maids were busy putting fresh sheets on a massive bed with four spindle posts carved with flowers. The wooden headboard was also carved with more flowers, painted in an array of bright colors, as though a garden had magically grown from the wood. She wanted to reach out and touch it. Bridget fancied for a moment how long the work must have taken to carve such a beautiful bed. She was almost tempted to try carving something like that herself.

"This is where ye'll stay," Mrs. Story said with a little smile. "'Tis one of his lordship's favorite rooms in the house."

Bridget noticed her cloth bag resting on the floor by the bed and snatched it up before one of the maids could nick anything from. She clutched it protectively against her chest.

"How many do I share this with?" Bridget asked. She bet she could sleep with at least another three girls on that bed, but she would prefer to sleep on the floor if it was more than that. She tended to stretch her hands and feet out when she slept sometimes and didn't want anyone boxing her ears in the middle of the night when she accidentally bumped someone.

"How many?" Mrs. Story echoed in puzzlement.

"Yes. How many of those girls do I have ta sleep with in this room?" She nodded her head at the maids.

The young women paused in their task of smoothing a satin rose coverlet over the bed and then burst into giggles.

"Oh... I see," Mrs. Story sighed. "Mrs. Ringgold, ye'll not share this room with anyone but yerself. Ye'll sleep in that bed alone."

"Alone?" *In that huge thing?* Bridget started to laugh at the ridiculous notion, but when she realized Mrs. Story wasn't laughing with her, she stopped. "It's all my own? Truly?"

"Yes. Now leave yer bag by the bed. No one will steal anything, I assure ye. And come over here." She opened a door that blended into the wall by using a small latch and led Bridget into another room. This chamber was much smaller and had no bed. There was a large copper tub, with steam rising off the surface of the water inside.

"Is this where we'll wash me clothes?" she asked as she clutched the collar of her shirt.

"No, this is where we wash *ye*, love."

"Me?" Bridget shrieked and started to back away, but two of the maids were already there to block her exit.

"Yes, Miss Ringgold. If we are to make a lady of ye, that means you must bathe. Fine ladies do not smell of stables or pigsties. Nor do they have an inch of dirt on their skin."

"Then give me a cloth and a bowl of water. I'll drown in that! I'm not using no tub." She stared at the large, steamy copper contraption. It could swallow her whole body inside it.

"No, ye won't and yes, ye are." Mrs. Story grasped Bridget's arm, and suddenly her clothes were being tugged off by the maids until she was nearly naked.

Bridget let out a bloodcurdling scream.

TRYSTAN JOINED HIS FRIENDS IN THE BILLIARD ROOM, where Kent and Graham were already playing. He walked over to the drink tray resting on the sideboard and prepared himself a glass of scotch.

"I trust both of you are settled in?" he asked.

Graham nodded as he bent to line up his shot. "Yes, thank you. Chavenage always takes good care of us."

Trystan hid a swell of pride. He had chosen his staff well, and they never disappointed him. He couldn't wait to see how Mrs. Story dealt with the tavern hellion.

"Where's the girl?" Graham asked.

"Being shown into her room and taking a hot bath. Mrs. Story usually prepares one for me when I return from my journeys, but the girl needs a good scrub more than I do."

Trystan sipped his scotch and enjoyed the taste of the expensive liquid burning the back of his throat. Then he retrieved a cue stick and joined his friends. But before he could start a round, a scream from upstairs echoed down the corridor.

"Bath is ready," Trystan said, half to himself.

"What the devil is that?" Kent asked.

"I'm sure it will stop any moment," Trystan said with confidence.

Only it didn't. With a growl, he thrust his cue at Kent.

"Excuse me a moment." He stopped out of the billiard room and hastened up the stairs, following the sounds of screams and splashes. A battle seemed to be occurring in the room he had given the girl. He entered the bedchamber and headed straight to the dressing room door, pounding his fist against it.

"Mrs. Story, are you all right?"

There was another screech and he heard Mrs. Story bellow like a bear.

"Sounds like a bloody zoo," he muttered to himself, then shouted, "I'm coming in!" and opened the door.

The dressing room floor was soaked in water. A bar of soap drifted lazily along the puddle of water past the copper bathing tub. Two of his upstairs maids stood in the corner, drenched clear through to their petticoats. Mrs. Story was braced over half the tub, wrestling with Bridget, who still wore that dirty white shirt of hers.

"Stay still, you ridiculous girl!" yelled Mrs. Story.

"Get your hands off me!" Bridget's face was streaked with dirt, which had only just started to loosen and drip down her face. She looked an absolute fright.

"Everyone out for a minute, *please*," Trystan growled.

The maids needed no convincing. They nearly tripped over each other trying to escape. Mrs. Story reluctantly released Bridget, straightened, smoothed her hair back into place, and marched past Trystan, chin held high. He closed the door behind him and stared at Bridget, who sank deeper into the soapy water when she realized she was alone with him.

"She was attackin' me!"

He took two steps toward her and held out a hand. "You will take off that shirt at once."

She removed the shirt and held the dripping bit of cloth out to him in a trembling hand. The second he gripped it, she ducked her bare arm back into the white soapy water as she curled her arms around her bent knees, hiding what little he might have glimpsed of her body.

"Now, you *will* allow Mrs. Story to wash you until your skin is pink as a peach. Then you will put on the clothes she gives you, and I will hear no more screaming. Is that understood?"

Bridget gulped. "But milord, she—"

"Tonight, you will feast on wonderful food. You will be so full you might need to be rolled out of the dining room. Then you will be tucked into that bed in the other room and sleep so deep that you won't even dream." He softened his tone, realizing he might need to use reason upon the unreasonable. "Bridget... you have been gifted a warm bed and meals for the next month. If you are too much of a fool to see that as the gift it is, then you will be shown to the nearest village and given enough money to get back to Penzance so that you may sort out your rather grim fate on your own."

He stepped closer to the tub. "I paid that man who calls himself your stepfather fifty-five guineas to release you into my care. Do you know why?" Bridget shook her head. "Because he is the sort of man who has no qualms about *selling* you. Men like him will force girls like you to do what they want, or they will sell you to others who will."

"To a man like you."

Trystan barked a laugh. "Hardly. A man like me has no interest in a woman like you. Not for *those* reasons." He crouched down by the side of the tub. "I paid him, but *not* to buy you, although I'm sure your stepfather sees it that way. No, I *invested* the money. I have invested it in *you*, Bridget." His voice softened a little, but he held her gaze. "If you become a lady and fool everyone at Lady Tremaine's ball, you will become a free woman of means. Imagine that for a moment."

He didn't miss the way goosebumps rose on her skin, or how she trembled a little. "You can marry well or rent a place to live in a safe town and start a proper life. If you're clever, you may even find a way to help other girls as I have helped you. Take my lessons seriously, and you shall take the wardrobe, the training and the nice bit of money I shall give you at the end as a payment for your part in this wager. Do you understand?" He didn't want this girl to focus on the way he'd paid for her like property. He wanted her to focus on her future, on the fact that she was in charge of her destiny now and could change her fate for the better if she only stopped fighting him.

The naked young woman in the copper tub stared at him with lavender eyes, and for a moment he saw past the dirty scamp she was to the creature which lay inside her, one that held such an exquisite fire to live a life of meaning and passion. Yes, *that* was the woman he had bet his money on.

"I—I understand, milord." Her lavender eyes were large and luminous, and he forgot what he'd been saying as his heart gave a strange little flutter in his chest. He gave himself a little shake to clear the flowery feeling from his head.

"Good. Now, Mrs. Story will come back in and help you. Once you get used to bathing, you might find you like it. The hot water eases the ache of weary, tight muscles and gives you time to reflect on your day in peace and quiet. It's a privilege to experience a thing that many others never will. Please be more respectful of my staff who provide such a thing for you."

Bridget's brows rose a little, and he could tell by the guilt-stricken look on her face that he'd made an impression on her.

"Very well. I'll leave you to Mrs. Story, and we shall see each other for dinner in a few hours." With that, he left Bridget alone to think while he returned to his game of billiards, assured he would have peace at last.

BRIDGET DIDN'T MAKE A PEEP OF PROTEST WHEN MRS. Story returned. She allowed the housekeeper to rinse her hair, wash her face with a cloth and scrub the rest of her body, even the bottoms of her feet, which tickled enough to make her laugh. Trystan had been right. The hot water was terrifying at first, but now it felt rather wonderful. She was limp as a rag, and it was a delightful feeling.

"We'll have yer hair cut fashionably tomorrow. I'm rather good with scissors," Mrs. Story bragged, but she said it with an amused chuckle when Bridget wrinkled her nose.

Bridget didn't care about her hair. It was a nuisance. The few times she'd tried to cut it with her little knife, she made a mess of it so she'd let it grow, which was almost as annoying. It now reached the middle of her back.

"There now," Mrs. Story said. "It's not so bad, is it, love?"

"No," Bridget mumbled.

The housekeeper retrieved a large towel from the washstand in the corner and held it up. "Stand up and wrap this around you."

As Bridget stood, the chill in the air clung to her skin, making her shiver. She took the towel and wrapped it around herself like a cloak, glad to feel warmer.

"Step out onto this so ye don't slip." Mrs. Story laid another towel down on the floor. "Then follow me."

She followed the housekeeper into the bedchamber and sat where instructed in front of a vanity table. Mrs. Story used a comb to untangle the knots in Bridget's hair, which took a long time, then she showed her the clothes she had brought for Bridget to wear.

It took the housekeeper several minutes to demonstrate all the bits of underclothes before Bridget felt confidant she knew how to wear them. She dried off and let the housekeeper help her into the clothing. She did not like the way the petticoats rustled around her legs or how the skirts hindered her walking. She'd never be able to dash about, the way she did in trousers. However, when she finally caught a glimpse of herself in the looking glass, she blinked in surprise.

She looked... well... almost pretty. Her hair was still a little wet, so Mrs. Story had braided it and twisted the braid into what the older woman called a chignon on the back of her head before securing it with some hairpins. The blue gown she was given was a simple affair by toff standards according to the housekeeper, but Bridget thought it was the loveliest gown she'd ever seen. It was a beautiful color and did something rather enchanting to her eyes. She'd never seen them shine so bright before, nor had her skin looked so luminous.

"Now ye look like a lady and a right pretty one," Mrs. Story said with a smile. "Let's get ye downstairs and surprise those silly men, eh?"

Bridget took one more peek at herself and bit her lip before she smiled back at the housekeeper and nodded. She barely remembered the last time she'd worn a dress... It had to have been about the time her mother died.

As they descended the stairs, Bridget felt vulnerable in a way she'd never felt before. She clutched her skirts in one hand, so her feet could find the steps easier in the little black slippers she'd been lent by one of the maids. The baggy masculine clothing she'd always worn before had made her feel safe, hiding her femininity. Now she felt she had no way to hide at all.

"My lord," Mrs. Story said to Trystan and the others once they reached the dining room.

Bridget ducked behind the housekeeper, rigid with dread at how Trystan might react to her appearance. She did not want to be yelled at again.

"Where's the little cat?" Trystan asked.

"Hiding behind me, I suspect." Mrs. Story turned and stepped aside, forcing Bridget to face the three men who lingered by the large mahogany dining room table.

They all stared at her and continued to stare for so long that she wondered if she'd grown a second head or something. Graham finally broke the silence by dropping the glass of brandy he was holding. It hit the floor, the liquid splattering all over the carpet.

"Christ!" Graham picked up the glass, blushing. "She cleaned up all right, didn't she?" he said to Trystan. "Assuming she's able to learn your lessons, you might just win, blast it!"

Kent elbowed Graham in his stomach. "Miss Ring-gold, please allow me." He walked over to one of the chairs that had a place setting in front of it. He pulled back the chair and gestured for her to sit. She stole a glance at Trystan, who was watching her with an intense but approving look. He nodded encouragingly, and she sat down in the chair before Kent pushed her in and then took the seat beside her.

Trystan sat at the end of the table, and Graham chose the chair across from her. The four of them occupied only one end of the vast dining room table, leaving over a dozen other seats empty.

"Do you usually dine with lots of people, milord?" She nodded at the mostly empty table.

"Not often. But a few times a year, I host a country house party and we fill up every chair," Trystan said.

Bridget turned her focus to the elaborate place setting. She had two glasses, several forks, knives, and spoons. When a footman placed a bowl of soup in front of her, she discreetly watched Kent. She was used to simply lifting the bowl up to her mouth, but she had a feeling with all the spoons lying about, she'd be chastised if she didn't use one. He took the farthest spoon away from the bowl. She reached for her own spoon in the same spot.

"Now, you should always work your way from out to in," Trystan explained. "The servants will only lay out the silverware needed for your various courses. We'll talk more on dining habits tomorrow. Tonight, you will simply mirror Kent or myself. Pay close attention to the type of silverware we use when we eat certain foods. If you have questions, you may politely interrupt to ask, but you will do so properly. If you speak with incorrect grammar, I will correct you and you will repeat the question appropriately."

"Yes, milord."

"*My lord*," Trystan corrected, enunciating.

"*My lord*," Bridget mumbled. Trystan arched a challenging brow until she repeated the correct response more clearly.

"Good. Now you may enjoy your soup."

Bridget decided to forgo any questions so she could focus on eating correctly, and more importantly, eating enough. She wanted what Trystan had promised her, a belly so full that she would have to be rolled out of the room. The soup was delicious, but she had no idea what kind it was. The next course was some sort of game bird served with hearty potatoes. That was a fine course indeed, and she loved the taste of it so much she nearly abandoned her silverware to pluck the bones off the plate and chew the last bits of meat off them. But she caught Trystan watching her, his eyes sharp as a hawk's. He kept up his share of the table conversation with ease, yet rarely took his eyes off her.

By the time dessert was delivered— a soufflé, as she was told in a whisper by Kent—her belly was definitely full and the stays that she been forced to wear were pressing against her ribs and back.

She was terribly tired. Her fight in the bath and the last day or so of being a bundle of nerves had taken their toll. She covered her mouth with a fist to hide a yawn and, after a glance at Trystan, who was not paying attention to her, she put one elbow on the table and placed her chin in her palm and briefly shut her eyes. A little nap, just a minute, and she'd be right as rain...

❧❦❧

TRYSTAN NOTICED THE MOMENT HIS CHARGE FELL asleep in her chair at the table.

"Did she just...?" Graham began.

"No, no, this won't do," said Trystan. He was about to shout something before Kent held a finger to his lips.

"Hush. Let her sleep, Trys," he whispered. "The poor creature is exhausted. Imagine for a minute the constant state of fear and dread she must have had up until today. Now she is in a safe place with a full belly. Let her have this one night of rest."

"Well, I can't exactly let her sleep in this chair all night, now can I?" As his friends stood up, he was about to shake her awake so she could walk up to bed, but something inside him stayed his hand. He looked to

Kent, who cocked his head, telling him what needed to be done without uttering a word.

"Blast your soft heart, Kent." Instead, he gently slid her chair back and caught the girl up in his arms, cradling her against his chest. She didn't even wake at the movement.

"I'll put her to bed and see you both in the morning," Trystan told his friends.

Kent placed a hand on his arm as he passed by.

"Give me your word she's safe," Kent said.

"Of course she is," Trystan said. "You know my taste in women."

"I do, but men can stray from their taste for the sake of convenience," Kent replied.

"I am no cad. I made a promise to you. I won't break it," Trystan said, his tone hardening. Why on earth did Kent think that this little hellion tempted him? She frustrated him. A lover didn't drive a man mad with irritation.

He carried the girl up to her bedchamber and laid her down on the bed. He was tempted to undo her clothes himself and not bother his servants, but knew Kent would have a problem with that. So he rang the bell cord for a maid. As he waited, he brushed a single loose lock of hair back from the girl's face. Once clean and dry, her hair was silky and carried the faint scent of roses from her bath. He stroked a fingertip down her nose, which had a slight upturn at the end like an impish fairy.

The girl was going to be trouble, he could feel it, but at least he was going to be entertained.

An upstairs maid named Marvella appeared in the open doorway of the bedchamber. "Yes, my lord?"

"The girl's fallen asleep. Please help her out of her clothes and tuck her in."

"Yes, my lord." The maid gave a shy smile as she passed by.

Trystan left Bridget to the world of dreams, and he went downstairs to his study to plan the lessons required to win his wager.

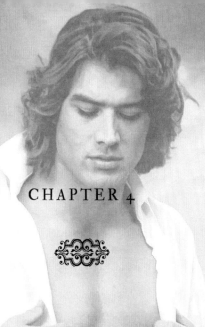

CHAPTER 4

Bridget burrowed deeper into her makeshift bed in the hayloft and let out a contented sigh. She was cozy as a bug nestled in a rug. Her stepfather wasn't shouting at her, and no one was making noise in the stable below her. It felt too good to be true—

Her eyes flew open. She stared at the plump white pillow cushioning her head. Then her gaze shifted beyond the pillow to the walls, which were painted with an array of wildflowers. Her hand held onto a rose coverlet. There was no sign of hay in sight.

Wait, no, this *is too good to be true...*

The memories came back to her slowly. She glanced around, taking in the opulent room. The last thing she remembered was having dinner with those three fancy gents. Had she fallen asleep at the dining table? She must have. She certainly didn't remember waking up to go to bed, so how—?

Her thoughts were interrupted as Mrs. Story entered the bedchamber with a tray of food balanced against one hip.

"Good morning, love. Time to sit up and eat. Then ye must come down and meet with the modiste in a few hours."

"The mo-what?" Bridget pushed back the covers as she sat up, but before she could get out of bed, the housekeeper placed the tray on her lap.

Eggs, warm buttered toast, and marmalade sat on the plate. Their tantalizing aroma drifted up to her nose, making her stomach grumble.

"The *modiste* is a dressmaker," Mrs. Story explained.

"Oh..." Bridget wasn't looking forward to wearing more dresses. They were pretty, but a bloody nuisance to walk in.

"Can I wear my trousers today?" she asked.

"It's dresses for now, love. If ye're to dance in a ball, ye need to be comfortable wearing them. Now, eat up. Tomorrow, one of the maids will bring ye yer breakfast and help ye dress."

Bridget ate quickly, not leaving a single crumb on her plate. Then she let Mrs. Story help her into the blue gown she'd worn to dinner. The moment she had her slippers on, she was escorted downstairs to the library. It was the most beautiful place she'd ever seen. Book spines with gold lettering glowed in the bright morning light.

"Wait here for his lordship," the housekeeper instructed.

The second she was alone in the library, she made straight for the ladder with wheels on the bottom and climbed up to get a look at the largest books on the highest shelf. She reached the top and gasped as she saw dozens of other bookshelves all in a row beyond the current shelf. She had never seen so many tomes in her life. Trystan had to be bleedin' rich as to afford so many books. It would have taken her a year of carving figurines to afford even one of these tomes.

The painted ceiling caught her attention next. She tilted her head back and saw dozens of angels playing among the clouds. Their wings had been painted with such care that it looked like she might be able to reach out and touch them if only the ladder were just a little bit higher.

"Bee—you—tiful..." she drew out the word in wonder. This library was heaven, and the ceiling had clearly been painted with that in mind.

"Like them, do you?" A deep voice startled her and she lost her balance, losing her grip on the ladder.

Bridget fell, but before she hit the hard floor, something soft cushioned her. Trystan grunted. She stared up into his eyes as she realized he'd caught her in his arms. The man had saved her from falling, like a dashing hero from the book of fairy tales her mother had read to her as a child. One of the few times she'd really been around books was as a child when her mother would read her stories.

"Perhaps try not to take flight next time. You're no angel yet." He let her down gently on her feet. She was still clutching at his chest, her fingers fisting his waist-coat. The heat of his body against hers set her on fire, and a masculine scent that clung to his clothes made her want to lean in and breathe deeply to memorize it. No man she ever spent time around ever smelled good like this. Most reeked of dirt and sweat. That funny tingling in her lower belly started up again. She thought of how close he'd been to her last night when she'd been as naked as a babe in that copper tub. Yet this felt different because he was holding her in his arms, gently this time, not dragging her out of a hayloft. Is this what it was like to be a lady? To have a fancy gent hold her in his arms like this?

"You told me you can read," Trystan said when Bridget finally forced herself to step back from him.

"I can. My mum taught me. She was very clever."

"I wonder if that's the reason." He stroked his chin thoughtfully as he studied her.

"What's the reason?"

"Your mother. Your speech slips often, but most of the time it's somewhat proper. Did your mother speak like those men in Penzance or more like me?"

"Like you," she admitted, not quite understanding his point.

"And your father? Your real one, not that brute from the tavern. What of him?"

"I never knew him. He died when I was a babe. Mum said he was a solicitor. She always said he was educated and a kind man. She loved him dearly. When he died, my mum had no other family or money, so she had to marry *him*." Bridget spat the word.

"You mean the brute?" Trystan clarified. Bridget nodded.

"Interesting. Well, that gives me hope, Bridget. You came from a home with proper speech. It's very deep in here." He leaned forward and tapped his index finger against her forehead. "All we have to do is *jostle* it out of you."

Jostle? He meant to shake her?

"There won't be *no* jostling," she warned in a loud voice.

"There won't be *any* jostling," he corrected.

For a moment they stared at each other in silent challenge before she spoke the words again correctly.

"Now, soften your vowels," he said. "Take your time

before speaking. Your accent is worse when you fly off the handle and start shouting like an angry peahen."

"*Peahen?*" she repeated in rage, even though she hadn't the slightest idea what a peahen was. "Are you saying I squawk like a chicken?"

"No, little cat, you shriek like a female peacock, or rather a female Indian peafowl, to be precise. But I suppose you've never even seen a peacock before, have you?"

"I have," she argued. "In a book. Big, pretty bird with a tail full of colors." She crossed her arms and raised her chin, proud of that fact. She doubted anyone else in Penzance knew what a peacock was. That book of fairy tales had plenty of wild animals and she'd learned their names. Lions...tigers...peacocks...elephants.

"Well, good. That's one less thing to teach you." He turned away from her then and walked over to a nearby shelf and selected a handful of books. Then he set them down on a reading table.

"You will sit and read to me. You will practice sounding like your mother. Imagine she is reading with you. Do you understand? We will practice this until the dressmaker arrives from the village."

Bridget reluctantly slid into a chair at the reading table and reached for the nearest book he'd set down before her.

"Does it matter where I start reading?"

"No, it doesn't. Choose wherever you like. I wish to better understand what I have to work with." Trystan, seeming restless, paced the length of the library as she began to read. She thumbed through the pages, seeking words she felt confident she could read aloud and stopped as she found a poem. She'd always liked poems.

"I wandered lonely as a cloud
That floats on high o'er vales and hills,
When all at once I saw a crowd,
A host, of golden daffodils;
Beside the lake, beneath the trees,
Fluttering and dancing in the breeze."

SHE PAUSED AND GLANCED UP TO SEE TRYSTAN'S pacing had slowed. He seemed calmer.

"Keep reading." He waved a hand for her to continue.

"Continuous as the stars that shine
And twinkle on the milky way,
They stretched in never-ending line
Along the margin of a bay:

Ten thousand saw I at a glance,
Tossing their heads in sprightly dance."

BRIDGET CONTINUED TO FOCUS ON THE WORDS, thinking about how her mother would have sounded as she pictured the stars dancing in the sky just like in the poem.

"The waves beside them danced; but they
Out-did the sparkling waves in glee:
A poet could not but be gay,
In such a jocund company:
I gazed—and gazed—but little thought
What wealth the show to me had brought:"

MOVED NOW BY THE SPIRIT OF THE WORDS, BRIDGET continued with more confidence.

"For oft, when on my couch I lie
In vacant or in pensive mood,
They flash upon that inward eye

Which is the bliss of solitude;
And then my heart with pleasure fills,
And dances with the daffodils."

SOMETHING DRIPPED OFF THE TIP OF HER NOSE AND she wiped at it, startled to find it was a tear. For a moment, she had felt her mother there with her in that room as she'd read. How had she forgotten how beautiful words could be?

A hand settled on her shoulder and gave it a light squeeze.

"Well done. I believe I have an idea of all we'll need to correct in the coming days. Oh, don't look like that. Chin up. You did far better than I expected. Language and the ability to read and speak are gifts to be cherished." Trystan's words of praise were softly uttered. As she closed her eyes, she felt as if she were actually *dancing* with daffodils all around her.

"Choose another," he said more brusquely. "And this time, remember to pronounce the letter H. It's *heart*, not *'art*. Think of the sound when you laugh. *Ha, ha, ha.* Use that sound."

"I *did* say it with a *ha*," she protested.

"If you did, it was so faint none but a church mouse would hear it. Do not treat it like an apostrophe. I wish to hear the 'huh' this time, understood? Begin." He resumed his pacing.

Bridget sighed and read a dozen other poems, each time receiving new instructions from Trystan as to what to correct next, until they were interrupted by Mr. Chavenage in the doorway of the library.

"Miss Phelps is here, my lord."

Trystan nodded at the butler. "Show her into the drawing room and have tea served. We'll join her in a minute."

"Yes, my lord." The butler glanced at Bridget before disappearing.

Bridget closed the book and stroked a fingertip lovingly over its cover. "Is Miss Phelps the dressmaker?"

"Yes, and not a moment too soon. I fear you are getting entirely too comfortable in that simple blue dress." Trystan started for the door. "Come along, little cat. We have a wardrobe to make for you."

She left the stack of books behind with a surprising reluctance. Now that she was surrounded by books, she didn't want to ever leave this room. After her mother died, Bridget had pushed away her desires for anything that reminded her of her mother, including books. Not because she wanted to forget, but because in order to survive, she had been forced to adapt her mannerisms and behaviors to escape the notice of the men that spent time at the tavern.

"Are you coming?" Trystan called out from the doorway.

She looked at him, studying him the way he always seemed to study her. She was arrested by the sight of his broad shoulders and chest that tapered down to his trim waist. He wore no coat, only a white shirt, trousers and waistcoat. The waistcoat was a deep burgundy with silver embroidery around the pockets and collar. He never seemed to wear anything overly fancy, but his clothes were as finely made as could be. His dark hair was lightly tousled, and he cast off an air of elegant care-lessness that was surprisingly seductive.

Bridget had never really thought about men in that way before. But now she couldn't seem to get it out of her mind. What would a man like him look like if he was naked in a bath and she had been the one to stare at him? She'd seen his bare chest once before, but now she was curious to see the rest of him. How would it feel to have him press her up against the wall the way she'd seen men do with women outside the tavern late at night? She imagined Trystan coupling with her in the dark like that, to see and *feel* all of his olive skin bared in the moonlight while he—

"Stop dawdling," Trystan said sharply, and she rushed after him into the corridor.

When they entered the drawing room, a middle-aged woman with dark red hair was setting out collections of colorful sketches on a nearby table. Behind her lay swatches of fabric in dozens of different colors.

"Miss Phelps." Trystan spoke with a gentle charm he'd never used with Bridget. The woman straightened and smiled.

"My Lord. Thank you for your kind letter. I'm delighted to help you with your cousin's young ward and build a proper wardrobe for her." Miss Phelps turned her gaze to Bridget, who was surprised to see the woman was smiling at her.

"Miss Ringgold, please come and sit by me. I should like to show you some fashion plates. I want you to be excited about your new wardrobe. A lady should feel confident in what she wears as well as comfortable."

⌘

TRYSTAN BIT HIS LIP TO HIDE A SMILE OF TRIUMPH. The moment Miss Phelps had uttered the word *comfortable*, the little wildcat was ready to eat out of the palm of the dressmaker's hand. He leaned back against the wall and kept out of their way while Miss Phelps showed Bridget dozens of fashion plates, patiently explaining her need for different types of gowns.

"You'll need day gowns, evening gowns, walking gowns, carriage dresses, riding habits, a court gown, and, of course, ball gowns. Then there are hats, gloves, stockings, shoes, boots, stays, chemises—"

Bridget's eyes went wide as the list went on, and Trystan couldn't stop grinning at his hellion's befuddled expression.

"I need all that?" she asked in a frightened voice. It held only a hint of the accent she'd had earlier that morning. His lessons were already paying off.

"Of course," Miss Phelps said as she shot Trystan a slightly confused look.

"Miss Ringgold has had very little opportunity to go out in society. The poor thing's been rather sheltered and isn't familiar with all of the types of gowns a woman out in proper society would need."

That comment brought Bridget's claws out, but she only scowled at him. He continued to smile like a doting older brother.

"Not to worry, Miss Ringgold. Step up on the stool, if you don't mind. I shall get your measurements and be on my way. I believe I can have most of your wardrobe ready in a week."

Miss Phelps produced a small stool with legs that folded out. She set it down and Bridget climbed up on it. She gave Trystan a glimpse of her dainty ankles when she lifted her skirts to let the dressmaker take her measurements. As he stared at those ankles clad in white stockings, a flash of fire shot straight through his body.

Not even when he'd been a much younger man had the glimpse of ankles ever affected him like that. He cleared his throat, and both ladies turned toward him, expecting him to speak.

"Er... I'll leave you to discuss the remainder of Bridget's wardrobe. Bridget, come find me in the dining room when Miss Phelps has finished."

He made a hasty exit and met his friends as they came in the front door. Graham and Phillip had gone riding that morning. Phillip leaned more heavily on his cane than normal, and Trystan felt a sting of sympathy for his friend. Riding was no easier on Phillip than walking. Movement of any kind pained the his bad leg.

"Glad to see you back," Trystan said.

"Where's the girl?" Graham removed his riding gloves and glanced about.

"Being fitted for her new wardrobe." Trystan invited his friends into the dining room for a light luncheon.

"How did things go this morning?" Phillip asked.

"Better than expected," Trystan said. "The girl's father was a solicitor and her mother, while not titled, was well educated. It's less a matter of teaching her new ways to speak than it is of reminding her of the old way she spoke before her mother died and she was forced to live with that brute at the tavern."

"Her mother died? That must have been very painful for her," Phillip said sympathetically.

"I suppose so." Trystan had honestly not given much thought to the girl's background or her feelings. The girl had been more of an experiment, a joke to play against high society. He made a mental note to attempt to think a little more about her feelings in the future, as long as it didn't slow down his ability to win the wager.

He, Phillip and Graham settled in the dining room for lunch and made small talk about their friends back in London, discussing the latest scandals Graham's older brother and his friends were involved in. As they were finishing up, Bridget rushed in.

"Have I missed lunch?" she asked, breathless, her cheeks flushed with excitement. Trystan couldn't help but picture her beneath him in a bed with that same expression as he made love to her. And just like that, he was hot all over again. He plucked a finger in the collar of his neckcloth to loosen it, and looked away as he counted to ten in Latin. Nothing like a dead language to kill a man's lust.

"Eat quickly, then join us by the stairs," Trystan said as he left the room. He needed to take charge of himself.

It's only that she's had a bath and a new dress. Any woman would be improved by such things. A man can appreciate an earthy creature and feel a little lust, but it doesn't mean anything.

She simply drew his fire, either from her wild behavior or because she simply drove him to frustration with her arguments. All he needed was a bit of relief. He was between mistresses at the moment and that, too, was part of the problem. He was not the sort of man to visit a brothel, at least not in rural Cornwall. It was a pity those Romani that visited his land last fall hadn't returned. He would have gladly talked his way into any one of those raven-haired beauties' beds. But they weren't here. Bridget was. He didn't like to admit that Phillip had guessed the girl would prove a temptation.

Damnation! She's an experiment. A wager. I do not want to take her to bed.

When Bridget showed up at the stairs, he had his weapon of choice ready. Graham and Phillip joined them, both keen to watch the disaster Trystan expected to face with his next lesson.

"Take this." He handed Bridget the slender book he'd been holding onto. She accepted it suspiciously.

"Are we to have more reading lessons?"

"No, you are to have *walking* lessons." He pointed to the top of the stairs. "Go to the top step, place that on your head and walk down to me without letting it fall. You may not touch the banister."

Bridget let out a long-suffering sigh, her lavender eyes narrowing as she marched up the stairs, grumbling.

"You know... I've never seen any woman learn to do this trick," Graham said. "Not even my sister Ellen, and she's quite graceful."

"Well, not all women need to practice grace. This creature has spent too much time swaggering about like a lad in a tavern."

"*Creature?*" Bridget cried out from the top of the stairs. "You bloody toff."

Trystan ignored her. "She must learn to soften her movements, as well as her words." He crossed his arms and shouted upstairs. "Now, walk down, Bridget."

The girl stood on the top step and placed the book on her head. It took some time to find the right angle to balance it. Then she took a step down. The book immediately slipped off and crashed to the floor. She let out an unladylike curse.

"Again," he commanded. "Without the swearing, if you please."

The girl tried again and again for over an hour and a half. She finally made it halfway down before losing the book, but by then she was trembling with frustration and exhaustion.

"Trys, let the girl breathe a moment. Even *I'm* tired of watching her," Graham complained. He was lounging on the bottom few steps, his legs crossed at the ankles, idly tapping the toes of his boots together.

Trystan walked up to the middle of the stairs and took the book from Bridget's hand.

"You're *rushing*, little cat. Each time you reach this spot, you move the slightest bit faster. That's what's causing you to lose the book. Do. Not. Rush." He tapped the tip of her adorable little nose with those last three words, then placed the book back in her hands.

"Once more. Truly concentrate. Then you may rest." When she started to turn away to go back up the steps, he caught her wrist gently, causing her to look back at him.

"Think of your mother this time. Think of what it means to float, as if you were descending to me from the top of the clouds. In this moment, you are a princess. You are grace and elegance itself. You have no reason to rush. The world is happy to wait for *you* to arrive." Then he released her wrist and returned to his position at the bottom of the stairs.

This time, Bridget took a slow, deep breath. She placed the book back on her head.

"The world waits for you," he whispered under his breath, and he sensed she heard him. The tension in her shoulder seemed to vanish and she held her arms out from her body only slightly as she began to descend the stairs.

Trystan held his breath, captivated, as he watched the girl float as if she was indeed riding a cloud down toward him. He could barely see her feet move, so gentle and controlled were her steps. When she reached the bottom, she slowly lifted one hand to catch her skirts and then she dipped into a curtsy. The book stayed exactly where it was supposed to be on top of her head. Trystan's lips parted in shock. He hadn't expected *that*.

"By Jove, she's done it!" Phillip cheered.

The spell broke and Trystan took the book from Bridget's head. She looked up at him with hope and excitement in her eyes, and damn him, he wanted to praise her until he lost his voice. But he couldn't do that.

"Er, yes. Well done. Tomorrow we start a new lesson. You may have the evening off, except for dinner, of course. I have letters to write. We must acquire invitations for you to a few places before the ball so that we will be ready for Lady Tremaine." Then he left Bridget at the foot of the stairs, ignoring the flicker of envy he felt as his friends showered her with praise. He knew now that he must keep his distance, lest he make a mistake and do something foolish like kissing the little hellcat.

Kissing her would be very bad indeed.

CHAPTER 5

Bridget could scarcely believe almost a week had passed since she'd arrived at Trystan's home in Cornwall. The days had flown by with startling speed thanks to the intense lessons that kept her busy from dawn to well past dinner every night. On the sixth day, she awoke to the sound of Mrs. Story and the maid Marvella whispering excitedly to each other.

Marvella had been helping her dress each morning, and Bridget had formed an easy friendship with the young woman. But she was still far too sleepy to understand why the maid and the housekeeper were fussing about in the room while she was trying to sleep.

"They're here, love. They're here! Get out of bed, silly girl!" the housekeeper exclaimed as she and Marvella carried in a stack of large boxes. Silly girl was, as Bridget now understood, a term of endearment the Scottish woman used for her, and she no longer minded when the woman said it. It simply made her smile and stretch.

Mrs. Story and Marvella set the boxes down on the foot of the bed. Bridget pushed her covers back before climbing out and joining them to examine what they'd brought.

"What's here?" She tugged on one of the fat red ribbons that bound up one of the large boxes.

"Your clothes, child! Miss Phelps just had them delivered." Mrs. Story chuckled and lifted the lid of the box.

Tucked in layers of delicate paper was a bright green gown embroidered with wildflowers in an array of colors. She glanced between the walls of her room and the flowers on the dress with more than mild curiosity. Trystan had offered his opinions to Miss Phelps about some of the dresses, but she hadn't remembered him asking to have one like this made. She wondered if he had sent extra instructions to the dressmaker.

Mrs. Story, Marvella, and Bridget unboxed the rest of the dresses. It took quite a while to put away the clothes in the tall armoire opposite Bridget's bed.

"May I wear the green dress today?" she asked the housekeeper.

"Yes, love. Marvella, she's in yer care now. I must

return to my duties." The housekeeper winked at them before she departed.

Marvella, being close to Bridget's age, had taken to caring for Bridget like a friend or even a sister. Bridget, having had neither of those in her life, found herself enjoying the experience. Marvella retrieved the gown and laid it out on the bed for them to sigh over again.

"Miss Phelps makes gowns just as well as any modiste in London," Marvella said. "I should know. I used to work at His Lordship's townhouse in London. I was always running errands to the different dressmakers."

"You left London to come here? Why?"

Marvella bit her lip, her pretty face suddenly a shade paler. "Well, let's just say I feel safer here in the country. Not all men are as gentlemanly as His Lordship. It's easy for a woman to get caught unprepared and... hurt."

Bridget understood far better than Marvella knew. "Did you get hurt, Marvella?"

The maid sniffled and wiped at her nose. "I almost did. I was running an errand, you see, but His Lordship happened to be coming home and saw me being accosted by a man in the mews a few townhouses away. He rescued me and took me straight home, after he... dealt with the man."

"Dealt with him?" Bridget asked in a whisper. "He killed him?"

"What? No! No, he just gave him a thrashing. The

man was moaning quite dreadfully by the end of it, and then His Lordship forced the man to apologize to me! Can you believe that?"

"No, I can't. He's always been such a bully to me."

Marvella sighed. "He's trying to make you a lady, to give you a chance any girl like me would die for. You see that, don't you? The chance you've been given? How good it is?

"Yes," Bridget reluctantly agreed. "So what happened after that man attacked you?"

"His Lordship offered to let me come here to work rather than in London. I was glad for the change. The young men here are sweet. One of the footmen here is even courting me, with flowers and all." Her cheeks warmed with a pretty pink color, and Bridget was glad Marvella was doing so well.

"Speaking of flowers, Marvella... Does Trystan, I mean His Lordship, like wildflowers?" She nodded at the dress that lay on the bed in front of them.

"Yes, he does. So did his father. Something to do with His Lordship's mother, I think. She was a gypsy, you know. Positively wild, they say, but in a wonderful way. The older staff who remember her simply adored her."

Bridget nodded. "Both of His Lordship's parents are gone?"

"Yes, his mother died when he was very young. His

father loved him so dearly and they grew even closer after her death."

Bridget had so many questions, but Marvella didn't have a lot of answers, because what Bridget wanted to know was private and personal to Trystan, and not the topic of gossip for his household staff.

The gown Miss Phelps had made fit far better than any dress she borrowed from Marvella, who was several inches taller than her. The maid helped her with her hair, pulling it back with a green ribbon at the nape of her neck. Mrs. Story had trimmed Bridget's hair several days ago, and the effect had been marvelous. Bridget had discovered it wasn't so troublesome to have long hair, after all. When her hair was clean, it turned soft and silky to the touch. She loved to sit and run her hands through it at night after Marvella had brushed it to a beautiful shine.

She also had to acknowledge that Trystan had been right about the hot baths. They were wonderful. She wished she could have one every night, but she didn't want those poor footmen carrying buckets of hot water up and down the stairs just for her.

"There, all done." Marvella smiled at Bridget in the vanity mirror's reflection as she rested her hands on Bridget's shoulders.

"I'm ready?" she asked.

Marvella laughed, her brown eyes twinkling. "I

certainly hope so. I can't think of more to do. You had better find His Lordship. I'm sure he has your next lesson planned."

The entire household had been informed of Bridget's purpose in being here, that she was part of the wager that existed between Trystan and Graham. Bridget still wasn't exactly pleased to be at the center of a game between two bored gentlemen, but she had taken Trystan's words to heart. At the end of this, she would have a different life, a *better* life. That was worth fighting for.

Bridget left her bedchamber and found the butler, Mr. Chavenage, walking down the corridor.

The butler bowed politely to her as if she were a grand lady. "Ahh, good morning, Miss Ringgold."

"Excuse me, Mr. Chavenage, where's Trystan—er—I mean His Lordship?"

"I believe he is in the dining room."

"Thank you." She proceeded to the dining room and found Trystan adjusting the placements of various silverware. Kent and Graham were also with him, both seated and relaxed, the picture of gentlemen of leisure.

"Ahh, good, there you are," Trystan said without even looking up at her. "We shall be revisiting dinner behavior today. Sit." He pointed at a chair and she walked toward it. Then she stopped, her hands resting on the back of the chair as she waited for Trystan to notice her dress. She had chosen the one that she was convinced he had designed, and she wanted to see the appreciation in his eyes for how she looked in it.

Kent glanced between her and Trystan before politely clearing his throat. "You look beautiful today, Miss Ringgold."

"Thank you, Lord Kent," she replied in her most practiced, cultured tones.

"Doesn't she look well, Trystan?" Kent prompted.

Trystan was hovering over the place settings a few chairs away and barely even glanced at her. "Of course she does. The gowns I had designed for her cost a fortune. It would be impossible for her to look poorly."

The callous comment hit Bridget like a dagger to her heart, but she wasn't a soft little creature like the ladies Trystan was no doubt used to. Years of living on the edge of society had made her tough. Yet the hard words that came to her lips died before she could say them. She remembered what she had been promised at the end of all of this if she behaved. Shouting at the foolish man would have made her feel better, but it wouldn't help her achieve what she needed. If she didn't know better, she might even have thought this was a test to get a rise out of her. Unfortunately, Trystan truly was *that* oblivious to the feelings of those around him.

"Sit, little cat." Trystan finally turned his attention on her. "We have a dinner party tomorrow evening at my great aunt's home near here. I need to be sure that you can handle the dinner. Let's begin your test."

She slid into the chair and waited for him to begin. He started to pace as he so often did. She'd never met a man with so much energy, but it was an energy that drove him to restlessness.

"You have just received an invite to dinner in two weeks. How soon do you send your reply and why?"

"I send my reply within a day because the mistress of the house will need advance notice to have enough food prepared and the table set for the appropriate number of guests."

Trystan nodded in approval. "Now, it's the night of the dinner. How soon or late do you arrive?"

"It is best to arrive about fifteen minutes before the..." How had Trystan phrased it? "Allotted hour for dinner?"

"And what if, by some misfortune, you are late?" Graham cut in with a twinkle of mischief in his eyes. He was seated across from her and was leaning back in his chair, one arm draped around the chair next to him.

"I..." She hadn't studied much about being late because Trystan had drilled it into her that she wouldn't *dare* be late. She continued more confidently. "A lady could perhaps be late up to half an hour? But a gentleman cannot be late at all. It's inexcusable."

Graham seemed mildly disappointed that she knew

the correct answers. "Shame on you, Bridget. You aren't supposed to be this clever."

Bridget didn't think she was being clever. It was simply logical to remember that women were given a bit more leniency in social appearances than men. Her lessons had shown her how long it could take to get dressed compared to men, so if they were a little late due to issues with their wardrobe, that seemed acceptable.

Trystan resumed his line of inquiry. "Bridget, when you arrive at the home where you are attending dinner, which room do you go into first?"

"The drawing room."

Trystan braced his hands on the back of the chair next to Graham, who was forced to drop his arm from it. "And who goes first?"

"Who goes into the room first?" Bridget fidgeted in concern. She hated remembering the order of preference for entering a room. It was difficult because it changed every time depending on who was present at the time.

"Yes."

"The ladies enter first, and it is considered poor behavior for a lady and gentlemen to enter side-by-side."

"And?" Trystan's gaze focused intensely on her face, making her squirm further. Sitting still was so difficult when he looked at her like that. "How is the order of entry determined? What order do they go in?"

"Yes, tell us this," Graham interjected. "If you have

Trystan, Kent and me in the drawing room and it's time to go into the dining room, who enters the dining room first?" He grinned like a wolf who had spied a lone sheep on a hillside with no shepherd about.

"Who would go first among the three of you?"

"Graham," Kent warned, "she won't have to know that—"

"I suppose that it would be between the two earls as to who would enter based on either their age—older in age first—or perhaps the gentleman who has been an earl longer?" She tried to ignore the rush of panic she felt by guessing. "But I do know that of the three men" —she stared at Graham with a little more pleasure now —"you would be *last* as the gentleman with no title."

Kent burst out laughing at the sour expression on Graham's face. "She's right. Graham, tell her she is."

"She is," he muttered.

Even Trystan was smiling, and Bridget preened a bit.

"Trystan, who would go first between us?" Kent asked once he stopped laughing.

"I actually don't know. We've always just made a decision in the moment, haven't we?" Trystan observed with a soft chuckle. "I may have to consult my book on *Etiquette for Gentlemen*."

"You do that," Graham snorted, his good humor restored. "Now, aren't we supposed to do dance lessons today? Dining conventions are *so* tedious."

"Later," Trystan said. "Now, Bridget, what are the two types of dining customs?"

"Er... they are *á la russe* and *á la française*."

Trystan nodded at the table of empty plates set out on the sideboard. "And what are the differences?"

"The *á la française* has only three courses. They would be laid out in a specific pattern on the table. There would be soup, fish, and meat. Entrées would be first, then meat, then dessert is third. For *á la russe*, it is simpler, with the dishes laid out on the sideboard. Servants will bring the food to the guests, who will serve themselves before the dish is taken to the next guest. There are less dishes served in each course, but more courses are served overall."

"*Fewer* dishes," Trystan corrected. "Dishes are countable. Now, let's say you are given bread." He reached for a vase of flowers on the table and plucked a large bloom off one of the roses and placed it on the plate in front of her.

She plucked up the flower, moving it to her left. "I take it and move it to my left side."

"And do you cut it with a knife or tear it apart with your hands?" he asked.

This was a trick question. Logic suggested tearing with her hands was uncouth, but in this case, it was actually the opposite. The knife was considered inappropriate.

"I rip it in half with my hands."

"Good, and what two topics are forbidden to discuss during dinner?"

"Religion and politics."

"Good lesson for life, really," Kent said, half to himself.

"Correct," Trystan praised. "Now let's have luncheon and practice everything you've learned. After that, we'll begin our dance lessons," Trystan said before he rang for the butler to bring them lunch.

⚜

"SHE'S DOING VERY WELL FOR ONLY ONE WEEK," KENT said to Trystan as they entered the small ballroom that graced the west wing of his family home.

"She is, but there is much that can be thrown at her that we can't plan for. I must try to think of everything." Trystan knew how unpredictable dinners could be, despite the rules they were all taught to follow. It would be worse if one of the guests smelled blood in the water, as it were. There were those who, if they suspected something was not quite right with Bridget, would test any sign of weakness in her facade.

"You never complimented her this morning," Kent said. The tip of his cane tapped softly on the floor as they followed Graham and Bridget into the ballroom.

Trystan's gaze roved over Bridget's figure. She had chosen to wear a dress that he had added to Mrs. Phelps' order shortly after their meeting. He had made a few additions based on his own preferences and what colors he thought suited her best. Green made her eyes glow, and he did adore flowers on a woman's gown. In his eyes, women and flowers shared a sacred connection. Perhaps it was his mother's gypsy blood, but because of her, he'd seen women and nature as intrinsically linked and therefore believed a woman should be surrounded by nature's beauty whenever possible.

His mother had adored wildflowers. After she had died, rather than hide from her memory, he and his father had embraced that adoration together to remember her. They had redone several rooms in the house, including Bridget's room, to make it resemble a wild English garden.

"She looks perfectly fine," Trystan finally said to Kent. "Bridget doesn't need me to tell her that. She knows very well that gown suits her."

Kent looked up at the ceiling and let out an exasperated sigh.

"A small compliment here and there wouldn't go amiss."

"It certainly would. The little chit is already far too brazen. I do not need to add to her confidence. She has plenty of it."

"Does she?" Kent let the question hang in the air before he left Trystan's side and joined Graham and Bridget. Graham said something and the girl laughed, her tone full of delight. Something stirred inside Trystan. A woman's laugh was always pleasant enough to hear, but something about Bridget's laugh touched him differently. He couldn't help but think of long nights in bed with her, seeking her ticklish spots just to hear that laughter from her.

He dragged a hand through his hair and grit his teeth, shoving back the unwelcome rise of desire within him.

"Let's start with the quadrille," Trystan announced, his voice harder than he meant it to be, but it had the desired effect of breaking up the couple and getting them down to business.

Graham gave him a curious look but stepped back, allowing Trystan to stand between them. Trystan explained to Bridget how the dance worked, and he demonstrated the lady's steps.

"Kent, keep a rhythm for her," he suggested. Kent began to tap a beat with his cane.

"Graham, show her the gentleman's steps."

When he felt confident that she could try it, he let Bridget and Graham dance. Bridget concentrated hard and counted her steps, but after a while she relaxed and soon she was beaming triumphantly as she danced as well as any girl who'd studied with a master.

"Very well. You've mastered the quadrille."

"Trys, let's show her a few country dances, just in case," Graham suggested. "Knowing Lady Tremaine, she might ask for a few of those."

"Good point," Trystan agreed. Soon they were showing her quite a few silly but highly entertaining dances that involved a lot of hopping, clapping, and swinging about. Then he gave the girl a moment to rest and had Mr. Chavenage bring them some water to sate their thirst before they continued.

"Now, about ballroom etiquette," Trystan began.

"Er, Trystan, you forgot to teach her the waltz," Kent interrupted. "I know it's unlikely that she'll be allowed to dance it without permission from Lady Tremaine, but better to know it than not, eh?" Kent seated himself in a chair by the wall, resembling some benevolent knight from the days of King Arthur. He held his cane with his hands resting on top of the handle like it was a sword.

"I'll show her the waltz." Graham took Bridget into his arms and the girl stiffened at the sudden nearness to the man, stumbling along as he all but dragged her around the floor in his enthusiasm.

Trystan shouldered his friend out of the way. "I think you'd better let me show her."

He put a hand on Bridget's lower back, then placed

one of hers on his shoulder. At the brief meeting of their hands, something burned hot inside of him. He attempted to bury the feeling as he grasped her other hand in his. Her eyes widened a little.

"Move closer, I won't bite." He gave her a gentle nudge, moving his hand at her hip to around her back and pressing her close enough that their bodies almost touched.

"Now," he continued.

Her lips parted and her tongue wet her lips... lips that suddenly looked very soft and kissable. He'd never really thought about her mouth before, but now he was fixated on it.

"Now?" she whispered,.

He refocused on the lesson. "Now... right... The key is to be graceful and effortless. You do not want to appear like a dancing master, nor do you want to be rigid and count every beat. You want to dance as though you've danced all your life in a garden beneath the waxing moon, the scent of orchids in the air and moon-flowers blooming around you. Dance is poetry in motion, and you must become that poetry."

She nodded, a look of deep concentration softening the expression in her eyes. He believed she was *seeing* that garden he spoke of in her mind, and for one moment he, too, imagined that they were in a garden beneath the moon.

"What do we do next?" she asked, her husky whisper caressing his ears.

He swallowed and again forced himself to focus. "Follow my lead. One, two, three. One, two, three." He counted as Kent tapped the rhythm with his cane. Trystan began to hum one of his favorite waltzes as he took a step backward and she followed his lead.

After a few moments, he forgot where they were as they whirled together around the room. He held the fiery beauty in his arms and she looked up at him, her eyes never leaving his. *This* was the magic of the waltz. It allowed a man and a woman to feel the heat of each other's bodies, let them feel close enough that they almost shared heartbeats.

In that instant, Trystan forgot the wager, forgot everything but this woman in his arms. His lips were curled in a hint of a smile and her gaze was dreamy, as if she'd only ever lived atop a hilltop of the most exquisite wildflowers. She was luminous, her beauty beyond words, and that feminine mystery all women possessed clung to her like the stars clung to the night sky.

He was going to kiss her. He was going to find out just how those lips tasted...

Trystan leaned in ever so slightly, and Bridget's eyes closed as their noses brushed.

"Ahem..." Kent said the word quite clearly and rather loudly from behind Trystan.

Then reality crashed back in, and he released her so quickly she stumbled.

"So... now you know the waltz," he said matter-of-factly. *Distance.* That was what he needed to keep from kissing the damned little cat. "Kent, why don't you explain dance cards and how the master of ceremonies works?"

He hastily stepped into the hallway outside and leaned back against the wall, catching his breath. What the devil had he been thinking? He almost just kissed the little hellion in full view of his friends and—

And that was not acceptable at all. It didn't matter how perfect she danced or how she felt in his arms. It didn't matter how much he wanted to taste her lips and so much more. It didn't matter because he *couldn't* allow it. He could not have a dalliance with such a girl. For one thing, he had made a promise to Kent.

He also didn't want the girl to develop any expectations. If he kissed her, it might mean a promise of something in the future. This was why he never dallied with innocent young women. He much preferred courtesans as mistresses. Or lustful widows. They knew the situation was only one of mutual pleasure. It wasn't as though he wanted to take a wife—and taking one with her background would cause no end of grief for him *and* the girl. He could withstand the scandal, of course, but she would be ostracized by others once the truth came out, and never be invited to anything social.

His mother had suffered that fate and it hadn't been easy. As much as he loved to break the rules, often to do it simply for his own pleasure, having a woman, especially one he married, suffer that fate was something he was not willing to do.

Some rules, even I cannot break.

CHAPTER 6

Something was different. Bridget knew it, and it worried her. Yesterday, when she had danced with Trystan, she had lost herself in the moment and done as he had told her to. She *became* the waltz. She had been moonlight, flowers and music. And for one brief moment, Trystan had been right there with her, the magic of the waltz transforming them from two beings into one.

She had never experienced that before, except perhaps with her mother when she was young. They had been reading a book together about faraway lands with names like *India,* and the story had come alive like some wonderful kind of magic. Being connected to Trystan had been just as wonderful, but in a different way. There was something about dancing this way with him, feeling the heat of his body against her own. She wanted to dance with him again and again until she was dizzy from the delightful twirling.

But today, Trystan was avoiding her. When they weren't at lessons, he was locked away in his study with orders not to be disturbed. During her lessons, he was more abrupt in his dealings with her than ever. His distance shouldn't have bothered her. The man drove her mad, after all, with his commands and constant quizzing. Yet it did bother her, and it *bothered* her that it bothered her, and *all of this* was a *bother*.

"Men," she muttered as she stomped ungracefully upstairs to change for dinner that evening.

She was a nervous wreck, as she was about to meet Trystan's infamous great aunt. Graham had made no small number of jokes about the woman, her poor eyesight and even worse hearing. Trystan had endured the teasing with an amused expression, yet whenever he had spoken of his great aunt, he'd sounded rather fond of the old woman. Whether that was because she was his last close relative or because he genuinely liked her, she had no way to tell. Regardless, Bridget actually desired to make a good impression on her. But rather than give any helpful advice, Trystan had drilled her over and over on various topics about the weather, which was the only subject she was permitted to discuss this evening.

When she tried to protest, pointing out how dull she would appear if all she could talk about was the weather, Trystan had arched one dark brow in challenge.

"Oh? And do you know anything about the economy, philosophy, literature, or the arts?"

The hurt this remark caused her must have shown on her face, because he quickly amended his words.

"When we have more time, I'll teach you anything you want to know."

"Anything?" she asked.

"Anything. But since we do not have time for that tonight, you must stick to topics that require very little studying. The weather and someone's health."

Graham had unhelpfully begun a discussion on the different types of clouds, which only confused her greatly. She couldn't remember the difference between cumulus and nimbus. By the end of the luncheon, she'd become properly muddled and more than a little angry.

As she dressed for the dinner, she clung to her anger over her fear for as long as she could. Anger she could control; her fear she could not. Marvella chose a purple gown with Van Dyck sleeves and pale pink satin rosettes trimming the hem of her skirts. Bridget had designed the gown herself with Miss Phelps. She wore slippers to match the rosettes, and pink ribbons pulled her hair back in a loose Grecian fashion.

The effect was quite stunning. She was confident

even Trystan would find no fault with her appearance. Bridget still couldn't get over her image each time she saw herself in the looking glass. She truly did look the part of a lady. She only wished she *felt* like one.

When she came downstairs to meet the gentlemen for their coach ride to dinner, fear was beginning to win out, and she was doing everything to hide her trembling. What if great aunt Helena discovered she wasn't a proper lady? Would she be tossed out and forced to walk home?

Kent and Graham spotted her first. She could hear Trystan's voice outside as he spoke to their coach driver.

"Everything all right, my dear?" Kent asked when she reached the bottom of the stairs. "You're very pale."

"I am a little nervous," she admitted.

Trystan appeared in the doorway. "Nervous? You have nothing to be nervous about, little cat. You've been excellent in handling everything we've thrown at you, so stop your silly worrying. Come along. We mustn't be late." He walked out the door again and waited for her to follow.

Kent offered Bridget his arm, which she gratefully accepted. He escorted her to the coach, then Trystan gripped her waist from behind and lifted her up into the coach. She squeaked in surprise.

"Oh hush, I'm simply trying to get you in *quicker*,"

Trystan said as he gave her bottom a tap, which made her leap into the coach.

"Oh! Why, you odious—" But before she could lay into him, he placed a gloved fingertip on her lips and silenced her. Then, with a gentle hand on her shoulder, he pushed her down into her seat before he sat down beside her. She pulled the hood up on her dark purple cloak, refusing to look at him. She made conversation with Graham and Kent instead over the twenty-minute ride.

Halfway there, the coach rolled over a dip in the road and she was flung into Trystan's lap as the coach teetered to one side. Trystan caught her in his arms, securing her against him when she cried out.

"There, there. I've got you, little hellion," he said with surprising gentleness. Her arms were wrapped around his neck, and they stared at each other for a long moment. Then he cleared his throat and slid her off his lap. She went back to ignoring him for the remainder of the journey.

When they arrived at Lady Helena's home, Graham and Kent exited first, followed by Trystan. He once again caught her by the waist and lifted her down from the coach.

"Now, don't be nervous," he murmured. "If you feel stuck regarding what to do or what to say, just look to Kent or me. We shall help you."

"What if Lady Helena discovers who I am? She might toss me out."

Trystan tapped her nose with his finger. "She already knows. I told her when seeking to add you to the dinner party."

"She knows?" Bridget gasped in horror.

"Oh, she won't mind. She knows I am always finding ways to amuse myself. This is no different. She was rather curious about you and this whole endeavor when she wrote back to me."

Curious? Bridget wasn't sure that was as comforting as Trystan meant it to be.

"Now, come along and stop fidgeting." Trystan escorted her up the stairs to Lady Helena's home, an old stone manor house, much like Trystan's but smaller in size.

Lady Helena was Trystan's father's aunt. She was seventy-two years old and hadn't ever married. She had been given the house by her father, Trystan's grandfather, and managed it over the years as its mistress.

The staff welcomed them warmly. Bridget allowed Trystan to remove her cloak, and she relished the brief comfort of his touch on her upper arms. Then, nervously, she followed the butler as he escorted her to the drawing room. The men followed behind. Inside the drawing room was a small party of five guests—two couples at least two decades older than her and an older woman. It was this woman who stood, and Bridget went to greet her.

"Thank you for the invitation, Lady Helena. It is wonderful to meet you." Bridget dipped into a light curtsy.

"You're quite welcome, my dear. *Quite welcome.* Allow me to introduce you to my other guests."

"This is Mr. and Mrs. Babcock. They have come from the estate next to mine. And this over here is Mr. and Mrs. Rutledge. They are my neighbors to the south."

"It's lovely to meet you all." Bridget greeted the two couples the way she had been instructed.

She was relieved when Trystan, Kent and Graham made their introductions and they conversed easily with the guests, allowing her to fade into the background for a moment. She remained quiet, absorbing the way the discussion flowed. It seemed to come so easily to everyone, especially Trystan. Despite his often brusque demeanor with her, he was charming and smooth with his great aunt's guests.

Bridget took advantage of the conversation not being directed at her so she could study Trystan's aunt. Despite the woman's age, she looked younger than Bridget had expected, given Graham's jokes, and appeared rather spry for her age. She did have a small ear trumpet in her lap and held a quizzing glass up frequently, peering through it at everyone, but she was not the old, clueless woman Bridget expected to meet. When Lady Helena turned that quizzing glass on her, she saw the cunning gleam in the woman's eye.

"Come here, my dear." Lady Helena waved Bridget to an empty chair beside her. Bridget sat down, relieved that the others were still involved in their own conversation.

"Bridget..." Lady Helena tested the name upon her tongue. "Hmmmm. A lovely and strong name. That's good. You need to be strong to handle my grandnephew. He's a scoundrel, but if you outlast his troublesome side, you'll find he can be quite the gentleman."

Bridget would have argued her point, but she recalled what Marvella had said about Trystan thrashing that man who had accosted her.

"You need not be so quiet, my dear," Lady Helena continued.

"Er... my apologies, but I was told only to speak of the weather and other people's health. Are you well, madam, and do you think it will rain tomorrow?"

Lady Helena snorted. "I'm *old*, Bridget, that's enough about my health. And as for the weather, I don't leave the house, so I rather don't give a damn. What I want to know is how you ended up here with my grandnephew. He told me that you were under his tutelage for language and lessons in etiquette. But knowing Trystan as I do, there is more to it than that."

Bridget shot a glance at the other guests, who had gathered at the far end of the room to talk.

"Don't you worry about them. They can't overhear us from over there."

There was something about Lady Helena that Bridget trusted immediately.

"Well, it's a rather long story."

"I did mention I'm old, didn't I? Try the short version."

"Well, Trystan found me working in a tavern in Penzance and bet his hunting lodge that he could convince everyone I was a lady."

"He *what*? I suppose you had better give me the long version, after all."

Bridget told Lady Helena her story and managed to finish just as the butler announced dinner was ready.

Lady Helena reached over and squeezed Bridget's hand. "We shall talk more on this later."

Bridget glanced at Trystan. It seemed her test was about to officially begin. She let Lady Helena lead the women into the dining room, and she was last before the gentleman queued up behind her. Trystan was the first to enter after her, and his hand briefly touched hers, giving it the faintest squeeze. She was so startled by the welcome but unexpected touch that she almost tripped.

She was guided into a seat by a footman and when she noticed the other ladies remove their long evening gloves, she followed suit and tucked them away. Then she placed her napkin in her lap and prayed she could make through the dinner without embarrassing herself.

❧❧❧

THE GIRL WAS DOING WELL, *SPLENDIDLY* IN FACT. IF HE hadn't grown so accustomed to her small tells, he would never have known how nervous she was. She presented herself as a poised lady whose manner was the very essence of calm. He had been seated next to Bridget by some luck, or more likely, his aunt's clever planning, given that Bridget might need Trystan if she ran into any difficulties.

As the first course was served, Bridget carefully emulated everyone around her and said very little.

"Miss Ringgold, you hail from Yorkshire, don't you?" Mr. Babcock inquired. He was the gentleman seated to Bridget's left.

"Yes," she replied, but did not elaborate further.

"Cold country up there," Mr. Babcock continued. "I hear they're looking into growing a larger textile industry there. More and more cotton, is what they're saying." Mr. Babcock waited for her to reply and for a second, Trystan feared she would freeze when she failed to find a way to relate cotton mills to the weather or Babcock's health.

"Er... yes. I believe we are hoping to match the Midlands in cotton production soon. Given that cotton makes up close to forty percent of Britain's exports, it would be wise to follow the Midlands' example and expand that economic growth. But my concern lies in the working conditions of these factories. We spent so much time and energy on the advancements of the technology in the mills, but we haven't taken any steps in making the mill *safer*. If we do not take care, the Luddites might rise again, as they did in 1779."

There was a heavy silence, and Trystan sat dumbstruck.

Mr. Babcock raised his glass to Bridget. "Quite right, Miss Bridget, hear, hear. If we better the working conditions, workers will safely produce more cotton, which will benefit us all."

Trystan, thankful of his control, managed to hide his shock. How did the girl know *anything* of cotton mills or Luddite uprisings? They hadn't covered that in any of their lessons. He felt someone watching him and glanced around to find his great aunt staring at him. She had that quizzing glass raised and her eyes were pinning him down. He quickly drank a full glass of wine and focused on the conversation, ready to dive in and discuss cotton mills if necessary.

The rest of the evening went well, with thankfully no new surprises. When the ladies left to return to the drawing room, the men stayed behind to smoke cigars and enjoy some port. Trystan felt confident Bridget could handle herself without him for a short while.

When the gentlemen rejoined the ladies in the drawing room half an hour later, Bridget was engaged in a lively conversation with the other women, who were listening raptly to her. Mrs. Rutledge was fanning herself and she looked both scandalized and delighted all at once.

Deeply concerned at whatever lurid tavern tale Bridget must be sharing, he started toward them. He only managed the catch the tail end of Bridget's story.

"And then islanders made the pirate lord their chief."

"What? The cannibals?" Mrs. Babcock gasped.

"Yes. But then he realized they were likely going to eat him soon, as they did all their chiefs, so he—oh hello, Trystan." Bridget smiled at him as he stopped close to the cluster of women. He couldn't let Bridget finish whatever story she'd been telling. Heaven knows how a story about pirates and cannibals would end if he let her continue.

His great aunt sighed. "Ahh, Trystan, I suppose you want to go now, and deprive me of Miss Ringgold's wonderfully entertaining company. Bridget, dear, you will have to come and visit me for lunch next week."

"Yes, Lady Helena," the girl immediately agreed. She thanked the older woman and followed Trystan as he escorted her to the hall where footmen waited with their their cloaks. Graham and Kent joined them, and they piled back into the coach for home.

"Well, that was well done of you, Trystan. Not a single incident," Kent said.

"It was indeed. We are proceeding well." Despite the rather lurid story the girl had been sharing, the women seemed to like her and the men had been impressed with her surprising knowledge of the cotton industry. Trystan smiled smugly. The wager was well on its way to being won.

"How the devil did you know so much about cotton, Bridget?" Graham asked.

"Yes, how did you know?" Trystan asked.

She looked between them, and gave a little shrug. "I may have worked in a tavern but I always paid attention to things people said."

"Well, you were quite brilliant," Phillip praised. "I think you could become a good economist with further study."

"You truly think so?" she asked him.

"I do, perhaps once we're all done with this ball business, Trystan could teach you more relevant things. You'd do that wouldn't you?" Phillip asked him.

"Yes, of course, if the girl wants to learn, I'll teach her anything." He was rather serious about that, and it was already giving him wonderful ideas about how his next wager could be to present Bridget in the house of lords disguised as a man and have her speak. The thought made him grin wickedly.

When they reached the house, Trystan was in a good mood and wished to celebrate. As a result, he forgot to assist Bridget out of the coach. When he turned back to help her, Kent had already helped her out of the conveyance. Bridget was quiet and he guessed she was exhausted from the evening.

"Go on up to bed, Bridget. Get some rest," he told her, then left for the billiard room with his friends.

The other two men had gone in ahead of him, but something made him pause and look back down the length of the corridor. The girl was *not* going upstairs. She stood in the hall, very still, her cloak still about her shoulders. She suddenly turned and walked out the open front door, leaving Mr. Chavenage to look on in confusion. The butler called her name, but the girl didn't come back into the house.

"Would you like a brandy, Trys?" Graham offered from the billiard room.

"Start without me. I'll return in a moment." He hurried down the hall toward his butler.

"My lord, Miss Ringgold has just left—"

"Yes, I saw, thank you." He stormed out into the night after his troublesome pupil.

The moon was bright overhead and the sky full of

stars, making it easy for him to spot Bridget as she walked down the gravel path that led around the side of his home. He realized at once where she must be going.

With a growl, he charged after her and caught up just as she entered the stables. He grasped her arm and pulled her to a stop. She whirled to face him, her expression alit with feminine rage.

"You should be in bed. We have more work to do tomorrow." He held her wrist and she pulled against him, trying to free herself, but the attempt was only halfhearted.

"I wasn't *ready* to go to sleep," she fired back. "I needed to clear my head before I bloodied your *bloomin'* nose." She was all fire and fury. Trystan was fascinated by this outburst.

"Whatever for?"

"Because you didn't tell me *I* did a good job tonight. You and the others were too busy congratulating yourselves. *I* made tonight a success. *Me!*" She yanked on her wrist again, but Trystan still held her firmly and she only succeeded in pulling herself into him so that their bodies collided. He caught her hip with his other hand, steadying her. The hood of her cloak fell back and her breath escaped in a rush.

Perhaps it was the fire in her or the scent of warm hay on a chilly spring night, but something unfurled and spread its wicked wings inside Trystan.

"Sass me again, Bridget, and you will regret it," he warned.

"Sass *you?*" She hissed and stomped on his booted toes. With a low growl, he spun her around and shoved her cloak aside as he pinned her against the stable wall and smacked her bottom. She shrieked in anger rather than pain, because he hadn't hit her hard at all.

"I'm not a child! You cannot treat me like one." She wrestled with him, but he kept her trapped between him and the wall.

"No, you're definitely not a child." He gave her another four light swats before his hand paused on her bottom. He was breathing hard.

His own body was as electric as if lightning had struck him. She looked over her shoulder at him, her eyes lit by the hanging lamps in the stable. He saw a sensual hunger in her, that ancient need that often could not be captured in words, but only freed by actions of the flesh.

"Keep looking at me like that and I'll kiss you," he warned, his voice rough and a little deeper than normal. He felt more a primal animal than man in that instant.

"You wouldn't dare," Bridget fired back. "You've made it quite clear you consider me beneath you."

"You should be so lucky." The burning match tossed between them had hit tinder. He turned her around to face him and pinned her against the wall a second time. He cupped the back of her neck, holding her head as he leaned down, his mouth slanting over hers.

Her lips were as soft as he'd imagined. Bridget's mouth parted beneath his and he delved deeper, his tongue seeking hers. She jolted in his arms as if surprised, and then softened. There was nothing more exquisite than a woman *melting* against him, but to have this woman felt richer, deeper somehow than any other experience he'd had.

He threaded his fingers through her hair, loosening the coiffure and all its carefully placed pins until her hair tumbled over the backs of his knuckles, tickling his skin. Lord, he loved her silky hair. He wanted to feel it caress his chest as she rode his body from on top while he lay beneath her.

The punishment he had intended with his kiss changed somewhere between Bridget's first soft moan and her second. He didn't relent in his kiss, but he gentled his ravishment of her mouth. Trystan slid one hand down her body to cup her bottom and squeeze it. Bridget rocked up on her toes and curled her arms around his neck, clinging to him. Emboldened by her reaction, he lifted her up and nudged his thigh between hers as he bunched her skirts up. She whimpered and gasped against his lips.

"Ride me," he encouraged as he urged her to grind

herself against his thigh by pressing his palm against her bottom.

Then he was kissing her again, and she responded eagerly. She rocked on him, rubbing herself against his thigh. He growled, hard enough that his cock felt as if it would rip his trousers apart. He gave her bottom another light smack and Bridget cried out, her arms tightened around his neck as she climaxed.

Trystan kissed her softly now, far more sweetly as she began to tremble. Had she ever been with a man? He'd never thought to ask her. He suspected she hadn't, and something in him warmed at the thought that he had been the one to show her how to find pleasure. When she finally stilled from her trembling, he tucked his fingers under her chin to make her look up at him.

"Are you all right?"

Those lavender eyes were losing that dreamy look and beginning to widen. "What the devil did you do to me? I—" Then she shoved him and jerked her skirts back down.

Now he felt his own temper rising. "What did *I* do?" He was still hard and desperately wanted to find his own release. The chit had the gall to be furious at him when she'd found her own pleasure?

Bridget's gaze dropped and she saw the effect their kissing had had on him. With a ruthless gleam in her eyes, she raised her skirts and brought her knee to his groin in a swift thrust.

His eyes bulged. Something had happened. It was bad. But it hadn't fully registered yet. He was barely aware of her rushing out of the stables and back toward the house.

He groaned, and took two steps after her, then fell to his knees. It was as if he was drained of all energy. Such an odd sensation, he thought, because he had no power to speak.

Then the pain hit. He swore he could see his own body as though from far above as he fell to his side and the true meaning of *suffering* hit him.

It was several minutes before he could think clearly again.

That hellion was going to be the death of him. But deep down, he knew he deserved that. And he also knew Kent was right. He was tempted, but he feared it had nothing to do with the convenience of her being here and instead was something else that he dared not name.

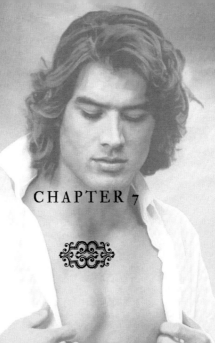

CHAPTER 7

Bridget studied the fine chestnut gelding the groom had brought out of the stables. Kent and Graham smiled at her puzzled expression. "He's for *me*?" she asked. "To ride today?"

"To ride *any* day," Kent corrected. "I bought him for you. He's a gift since you've been doing so well in your lessons. Besides, you ought to have a horse to get around once the wager is over." Kent's eyes twinkled as he leaned on his cane. The pain that so often shadowed his features faded beneath his joy and excitement. Bridget couldn't believe that he had bought her a *horse*. The quality of the beast alone told her it was an expensive creature that she never would have been able to afford on her own. She peeped beneath her lashes at Trystan, who stood close by, scowling.

She was the one who had the right to scowl, not him. After what had happened last night, she was the one who was furious. To spank her like a child was bad enough, but to make her enjoy it and enjoy what came after and then to be so bloody arrogant about... well, *everything*.

"*I* should've bought the girl a horse," Trystan grumbled.

"Well, you didn't. Nor would you have thought of it on your own," Kent said, his unwavering joy intact. "Bridget, come over and pet him so he can learn your scent." Kent urged her to join him by the horse. "His name is Beau. He's two years old and the most dapper prancer you'll ever see. I can't wait to see you ride him in Hyde Park."

"You'll be the envy of every lady and gentleman," Graham said. "This is a fine beast. I helped Kent choose him."

She reached up and petted the horse. The beast bumped her hand in greeting. She shot Graham an appraising look while she stroked Beau's nose. "I didn't think you wanted me to win your wager."

"Wagers aside, every lady deserves a good horse. Besides, even though I don't wish for Trys to win, that doesn't mean I'd want to punish you. You've been an awfully good sport indulging in our whims. You deserve

something for dealing with us 'spoiled fancy gents,' eh?"
He chuckled.

Beau's dark brown eyes stared into hers and she felt a
sense of peace wash over her. She'd heard that horses
were like that.

"I love horses, but I've never ridden one."

Trystan joined them, his face incredulous. "But you
lived in a bloody stable."

"I only slept there so no one could find me. Men
would get deep into their cups, and it's easier to kick a
door in at the tavern than climb a ladder. But I've never
ridden a horse, not once."

"Then today you will learn." Kent beamed at her.
"Riding a horse is a freedom that you will soon become
addicted to." He then turned to Trystan. "Doesn't she
look smart in her new riding habit?"

Her burgundy velvet riding habit had a matching hat
that perched on her head, decorated with a lovely
pheasant feather. She loved how she looked in it, but
hadn't realized that putting this on meant she'd be
getting on a horse. She'd been too busy spinning around
in front of the mirror, admiring her reflection like a silly
magpie.

"You know very well she does," Trystan said grumpily.
"Come here, Bridget. I will help you." He grasped her
hand and pulled her toward him. She was so focused on

the feel of his hand that she didn't realize he was lifting her up until her bottom plopped down into the saddle. She was suddenly frozen with fear as her legs dangled off the same side of the horse. She was sitting almost sideways on it, which didn't feel the least bit steady or safe.

"Bridget?" Trystan's voice sounded strangely distant. All she could really hear clearly was a ringing in her ears, and all she felt was the thud of her heart as it beat hard enough to break free of her chest.

"I..." She was too afraid to move, let alone speak. She sat fairly high above the ground, and the horse felt huge, powerful, *dangerous* beneath her body. What if it threw her off and then trampled her? What if it fell over and crushed her under it?

"Perhaps I should..." Trystan began, but rather than finish his thought, he mounted up behind her.

The feel of Trystan's strength and the support of being able to lean back against him settled her whirling, panicked thoughts like a murmuration of starlings landing upon the ground all at once.

"Better?" he asked.

"Y—yes. I was just a little frightened," she admitted, her voice still shaking.

"Don't be, little cat. I've got hold of you now. I'll teach you what you need to know."

Somehow their quarrel last night and the wondrous, almost frightening pleasure after that had changed her.

Not that she could say how exactly. All she knew was that she felt less upset with him than she had last night... and oddly more comforted by him.

Kent and Graham mounted their horses and began to trot ahead of Bridget and Trystan.

"Riding sidesaddle is a lesson for another day," he said. "Pull your left leg over, that's it, good girl. Lift your skirts up so you can straddle the horse. Since I'm using the stirrups, you just hold on to him with your knees."

She lifted her skirts and let her legs drop down the sides of the horse, then lightly pressed her knees into the animal's flanks, securing the grip of her body on the horse. It felt much more stable than the way she'd been sitting before, where she'd been half perched on the beast's back.

"Why do women ride the other way?" she asked him.

"I'm afraid you'd find it a rather silly answer," Trystan hedged as he nudged the horse forward with a light kick.

"Tell me."

"Society... polite society at any rate—" he began

"You mean *men*," Bridget cut in, having a suspicion where the subject was headed.

"Er, yes. Well, they do not think women should feel... how should I put this? They are concerned a woman might feel *aroused* by the motion between their thighs. And also, men can't see so much of the women's legs when they ride sidesaddle."

"Oh, that does sound silly," she agreed. She pictured so many women falling from horses because they had to sit in such an uncomfortable and unstable way. All because of what some *men* thought.

"I actually agree, but then again I think a woman *should* feel pleasure if they wish and I believe I have the right to enjoy seeing her lovely legs if she chooses to bare them." He chuckled, the rich sound rumbling from his chest into her back. Bridget liked Trystan when he was relaxed and not busy giving orders.

Graham rode down the road at a gallop while Kent kept his horse beside Trystan and Bridget as they walked down the drive that led away from the house. The avenue was lined with chestnut trees bright with new leaves that danced in the light breeze, the sun soft and warm upon Bridget's face. Despite the distant clouds, she could smell the clean scent of fresh rain and guessed that they would have a shower soon.

Trystan began his lessons again, and Bridget found this classroom on horseback preferable to the dining room table or the library. Despite her growing love of Trystan's books, she loved being out in the world far more.

"Now, we should discuss some behavior you will need to learn for when you are in town," he began.

"Where shall we start?" Kent asked.

"Walking, I should think," Trystan continued. "Bridget, are you listening to me?"

"Yes." She shot a little smile at Kent, who seemed to notice that she'd been daydreaming. He returned the secretive smile.

"There are fashionable hours to go to Hyde Park when walking and being seen by others in society is your desire. Between the hours of five and six o'clock in the evening..." He droned on about fashionable hours for various activities, and she stopped listening. It was only when he pinched her bottom that she jerked and sat up straighter and focused again.

"No walking alone as a young unmarried woman. You must have an approved chaperone with you. If you are married, you can walk with a companion who does not need to be a chaperone. Now, if you see someone you are acquainted with and you wish to acknowledge them, you must allow the person with the higher rank to acknowledge you first, unless it's a man. Even if he's a duke, *you* are the lady and you have the power to acknowledge him first. As a lady, you always have the right of recognition before any man. The only exception would be if the gentleman had long-standing intimate or familiar acquaintance with you."

This was a *little* more interesting than the rules of fashionable hours.

"How do I acknowledge someone?" she asked. She

doubted she would ever recognize anyone, but it was worth asking.

Her hands held lightly onto the reins of the horse now. Trystan's hands also held the reins, their fingers brushing occasionally as the horse walked along. Sparks of awareness danced up her arms. She tried not to think of his hands being bare of gloves and swatting her bottom, but the mere thought of it sent waves of desire burning in her lower belly.

"A lady will give a slight bow or an inclination of her head. A gentleman will bow and lift his hat entirely from his head. If he merely touches the brim of his hat at you, that is unacceptable," Trystan continued, completely unaware of her thoughts.

"Would you thrash a man who did that to me?" she asked in a teasing tone. Kent laughed.

"I might," Trystan said quite seriously. "Respecting women is the highest form of civility. You are the fairer sex and deserve such treatment to reflect that."

If Kent hadn't been there, she would have asked Trystan about whether spanking a woman and then kissing her the way he had was respectful. She'd love to see him react to that. The man would likely splutter about and then spank her again. She bit her lip to hide a smile at the thought. She was starting to realize that a frustrated Trystan was a passionate Trystan. Perhaps she'd been too quick to get upset with him. After all, she'd rather liked everything that had happened last night. She'd wanted to deny that at first, but now she couldn't.

They rode another fifteen minutes touring his lands before she spotted an old set of ruins half hidden in the woods.

"What is that?" She pointed at the ruins.

"Part of an old Saxon church," Trystan said.

"Can we go see it?" Bridget asked, excited.

"Go on, take her, Trys. I'll catch up with Graham." Kent urged his horse toward the distant figure of Graham still cantering across the field.

She and Trystan went on alone. When they reached the edge of the stone structure, he slid out of the saddle and helped her down. For a moment, his hands lingered on her waist and hers on his shoulders. She gazed into the warm whiskey brown of his eyes and once again was filled with a forbidden hunger for him.

"About last night," he said slowly, his tone soft and hesitant. "I must apologize for... for what I did."

"Spanking me like a child and then kissing me... and all that followed?" she asked. Neither of them moved. The air felt suddenly charged, as if a building storm was above them.

"Well..." His lips twitched as he fought off a devilish smile. "I only apologize for my *tone* when I spoke to you. I stand by all the rest, hellcat." Trystan released her hips and they walked toward the ruins. The way he said hellcat this time was less of an insult and more of an endearment.

"Yet you spanked me like a child!" she protested.

"That had nothing to do with treating you like a child. I know full well you are a grown woman." Trystan's voice deepened and Bridget shivered, but not from fear.

"Then what did it have to do with?"

Even though no one was around to hear them, she somehow knew her question was going to prompt a discussion of a forbidden nature and she glanced about. They stopped by the entrance, where there was a low wall a little higher than her waist. She knew he was stalling as he leaned on the crumbling stone wall and studied the foundations. Part of the structure still stood, but much of the rest had crumbled.

"Trystan, please, you must tell me." She stood beside him, raised her skirts and attempted to hop up on the lower part of the wall, but it was too high. After watching her frustrated attempts, he picked her up and set her down on the wall so she sat in front of him. He placed his palms on either side of her hips, their faces only a few inches apart.

The breeze teased a lock of dark hair across Trystan's forehead. His features held such a beautiful contrast between the hard planes upon his face and the wild softness of his thick, dark hair.

Unable to resist the urge, she reached up and brushed the hair out of his eyes. He caught her wrist, holding it gently. She wished that neither of them were wearing gloves because she wanted to feel his skin on hers. As if hearing her thoughts, he slowly removed his gloves, then hers. Then he stroked the inside of her palm with his thumb. The simple touch was seductive in a most hypnotic way.

"What we are teaching you, all of the manners and dance lessons, it's only half of what it means to be a lady. There is so much you need to learn about men and what men want. More importantly, you need to learn what you *deserve* from men."

"In bed?" she guessed, her breath quickening.

"Yes, but also in life."

"I don't wish to marry."

"Then you are indeed a silly creature," he sighed. "I don't wish to marry, but my station affords me that luxury. For you, it only closes off opportunities you would not have otherwise."

"Because it is a man's world," Bridget muttered.

"It is what it is," said Trystan. "Now, let's pretend that for one moment you dance in the arms of a handsome man at Lady Tremaine's ball and you feel a flutter in your belly..."

She recognized what he meant, that sensation that sometimes was so overpowering she almost felt dizzy.

But in her limited experience, he was the only man she'd ever felt that for. She'd not experienced it with Kent or Graham, and they were both just as handsome as Trystan.

"Society teaches you that women do not have or *should* not have any desires or pleasures. But that is a lie. Women's bodies are designed like those of a goddess. You are creatures born to feel the most exquisite of pleasures. Your body is a map rich with pleasurable destinations, and when a man and woman come together, it can be truly beautiful. It can be beyond anything you've ever dreamed. With the wrong man, it might be uncomfortable, unpleasant, and possibly even distasteful." He let go of her wrist to reach up and stroke the spot just behind her ear, which sent shivers down her spine. She squirmed.

"You still haven't explained why you spanked me," she reminded him.

His lips twitched.

"There are games men and women play, interesting positions they can try and toys to use..."

"Toys?" She couldn't imagine what he meant by that. "Like dolls?"

He chuckled sinfully and shook his head. "No, not like dolls." He took her wrists in his, encircling them with his own strong fingers until he was controlling her hands. "Imagine me holding you like this. You cannot escape me as I kiss you in places like this..." He leaned in to kiss her lips and then he moved up to her neck, nibbling and then nipping at her ear. He flicked his tongue along the shell of her ear, and she shuddered and gasped as a heavy throb between her thighs suddenly overwhelmed her.

"How does that make you feel, little cat? Does it make your thighs tremble? Does your secret place between your thighs ache for something you do not yet understand?" The naughty words whispered in her ear made her whimper.

"Y—yes!"

He bit the lobe of her ear lightly, but the little sting was too much. "Trystan," she begged, but she wasn't sure what she was asking.

"Do you know what you need?" he asked as his hold on her wrists tightened slightly. "When you feel your body under my control, to know I'm the master of your pleasure? It excites you, doesn't it? A good man will know how to give you what you need, like the occasional spanking. You need no master to command you to live your life, but you *might* need a man who proves he is worthy of your fire and your surrender."

"My surrender?" She wasn't sure she understood, but it was hard to think beyond the vivid, erotic imagery his words painted.

"When you surrender in those moments of pleasure,

you will become that man's master. *You* hold the control. A good man only appreciates his own pleasure when he's certain he's seen to yours." Trystan kissed the hollow of her throat and she threw her head back, gazing up at the storm clouds building above them. It was as though her arousal had built the storm, which any second would unleash itself upon them.

He paused in his kisses to whisper in her ear again. "But you must be careful, little cat. The wrong man would break you, not set you free."

"Trystan... I need... I need..." She wished she knew what to ask him for. "*Please...*"

He let out a shivery sigh of his own. "I have a confession to make," he said. She looked at him with pleading eyes as he struggled to admit what he felt. "You are the most irresistible woman I have ever met. You have no idea what you do to me."

She shifted closer to him in desperation. "If it's *anything* like what you're doing to me, then I have some idea."

He smiled, and it broke the last of her restraint. She squirmed on the wall ledge and spread her legs as wide as the riding habit would allow. His smile vanished, and he switched his hold on her wrists to one hand before he slid his other hand up her skirt to touch her where the ache was most fierce. She gasped as his fingers traced the folds of her sensitive flesh. His eyes darkened with desire as he eased a finger into her.

"Oh God..." She moaned at the foreign feeling of that gentle penetration. She loved it, no hated, no... she *loved* it. He withdrew his finger and then pushed it in again, deeper this time.

"So tight," he whispered, his voice raw with lust. "You'd grip my cock like a fist, wouldn't you?"

He lowered his head, his lips settling hungrily over hers as he continued to penetrate her with his finger while kissing her, and yet she needed more. Her soft pants between kisses deepened as he added a second finger to the first. He quickened the pace and his kiss deepened, his tongue thrusting in time as he showed her what pleasure was.

"That's it, little cat," he growled, "show me your passion, show me you *belong* to me, and I shall be yours." Something about the words, about belonging to him even as he held her prisoner... it was all she could take as that building hunger peaked. She shattered inside just as the skies above them let loose its storm.

She rode wave after wave of pleasure as Trystan continued to push his fingers into her, but far gentler now. He slowed his kisses and rested his forehead against hers. She felt a powerful connection spring into being between them as the rain pelted against their heated skin.

He withdrew his hand from her skirts and then lifted her down from the wall, but her legs shook so much that she didn't dare move. Trystan scooped her up into his arms and carried her toward a part of the ruins that still had a small roof. He set her down, then went back out into the rain and returned, leading her new horse into the high-ceilinged structure with them.

"We had best wait out the storm here," he said.

She rubbed her hands together, shivering from the rain that had soaked her red riding habit.

"Cold?" he asked.

Bridget nodded. Trystan came over and eased down onto the ground, then joined her and pulled her into his lap. He wrapped his arms around her, warming her with his body heat.

"Promise me that someday you'll choose a man who will see your value." Trystan murmured the words into the crowd of her hair.

"Someone like you?" she dared to ask.

The silence was a beat too long. "No, little cat. I'm not the one for you. There are far better men out there. Men who will set fire to your world with adventure and passion."

She laid her head on his chest, closing her eyes. She dared not say what she felt, but it was clear she was not the woman he wanted, not in that way. He was simply her tutor, nothing more. That realization chilled her more deeply than any spring rain could.

When the storm passed, they left the old ruins. She wondered if perhaps these ruins had once been a place for the old Celtic warriors to offer sacrifices, because it felt as though her heart had been opened upon the altar there, and left to bleed out.

CHAPTER 8

Trystan wasn't sure if the fleeting pace of the next three weeks had been a relief or a punishment. He had managed, through sheer determination, to stay away from Bridget in situations that could have ended with her flat on her back and him inside her. Trystan rather suspected it was Kent's blasted protective nature and watchful attitude that had truly kept him at bay.

That day of the rainstorm, when Trystan and Bridget had returned to the house disheveled and soaking wet, he had guiltily avoided his friend's inquiring gaze. Graham had teased him as if he had seen nothing worrisome in the time alone the two had shared, but Kent had instead become ever more vigilant after that day.

Now it was all coming to an end. Now was the

moment everyone had been waiting for, the night of Lady Tremaine's ball. After tonight, he and Bridget would be free of the wager... and of each other.

They had arrived at his London townhouse five days ago to settle Bridget into the city. She had been overwhelmed at first, but as always, she had surprised Trystan and adapted to the London's pace with ease. They had taken her riding in Hyde Park and let her eat ice cream at Gunter's. They'd taken her shopping for a dress suitable for Lady Tremaine's ball and, against Trystan's wishes, they'd also snuck her into Tattersall's dressed as a boy.

He hadn't wanted to risk her being discovered as a woman in that auctioneer house where females were forbidden, but later he was glad for the excursion. Seeing the girl's face as she'd walked among the rows of some of the best horseflesh in London had been worth it. She'd enjoyed every minute of watching the rich and powerful vie over the most amazing horses England possessed.

But all of those adventures had now come to an end. Only the ball remained, which was starting in the next half hour. The training they had pushed her through in the last month would be put to the test tonight. Trystan had prepared for this moment by putting on his superfine black coat, favorite gold waistcoat, and breeches. He now stood at the foot of the stairs, waiting for Bridget to join them.

"You know, I *almost* hope she wins tonight," Graham said as he tugged at the edges of his coat to straighten it out.

"She will win, I have no doubt of that," Trystan said with confidence. Even he would have believed she was a lady if he had never met her before tonight. He'd done a masterful job of putting her through her paces like any good racehorse in preparation for Ascot. He was thoroughly impressed with the progress she'd made. She had passed every test he had contrived and more.

"She will have us there to offer guidance," Kent said to Trystan.

"You know, Kent, it's rather unfair that you sided with Trystan. If I win, I won't invite you to my new hunting lodge for a full year," Graham said.

Kent clutched his chest. "Oh, how you wound me, old friend. But in truth, I didn't actually side with Trys," he said.

"Oh? Then whose side are you on, old boy?" Graham demanded of him.

"Why, Miss Ringgold's of course," Kent said as if that explained everything.

Trystan chuckled. The three were still teasing each other when Graham suddenly stopped talking and looked at something behind Trystan and Kent, his eyes as round as saucers.

When he turned around, Trystan for the first time in

his life simply forgot to breathe. The woman descending the stairs so effortlessly was a vision of divine beauty, so much so that it seemed a crime to even look upon her.

The silver gown had a glittering gossamer outer skirt that shimmered in the lamplight with every step Bridget took. At her throat rested a single chain with a star formed by a cluster of diamonds. Her hair was pulled up into a soft tumble of curls and small, matching diamond stars clusters were pinned into parts of her coiffure. It looked as if the constellations had fallen from the night sky and taken it upon themselves to bind her hair back with celestial care.

Trystan had pondered at length what her ball gown and hair should look like for tonight in order to create the right effect for the *beau monde*. But the idea he had in his head was no match to the flesh-and-blood vision standing before him. She wore two white gloves up to her elbows and carried a slender fan in one hand. Her other hand held onto the train of her gown as she descended the stairs. She studied their faces in silence, waiting for comment or criticism, but none of them, had anything to say. Trystan could only blink and continue to stare at her. He could have stared at her for the rest of his life.

Her lavender eyes settled on him. "Are we ready to leave?" A footman brought her a blue cloak and she wrapped it around herself just the way a lady who'd worn fine cloaks for years would. One loose curl from her hair caressed her cheek and he found himself jealous of that curl, wishing he could touch her skin the rest of the evening.

"Er...yes." Trystan finally found his tongue. He offered her his arm once she had donned her cloak. They walked out to the coach and he helped her inside, his friends following close behind.

"Are you ready for this evening?" Kent asked Bridget once the coach started toward Lady Tremaine's.

"Yes, I believe I am," she replied. Her soft tone was sweet, confident. To his surprise, Trystan found he missed the brash, outspoken, wild creature she had once been before he had taken her and changed her into this beautiful lady. She was poised and graceful with remarkably innocent eyes that reminded him of that time they had waltzed together, as though she had danced only ever in moonlight and surrounded by flowers. She was magnificent, yet at the same time, he wondered if he done something terrible by destroying the hellion inside of her.

He had planned to use her as a way to thumb his nose at his fellow aristocrats, and prove that anyone could be trained to act like they'd been born into high society. He'd wanted to show the *beau monde* that they were no better than a hellcat like Bridget was... but the truth was, he'd come to believe that she was better than they were. She was honest and fearless, and now he feared he'd taken both those qualities from her.

She's better this way. She'll have a future this way, a voice whispered inside of him. But the thought didn't erase his guilt or disappointment. The thing he had loved about her was that she wasn't fashioned from some clay mold, as other women in London seemed to be. She had fascinated him on every level. Bridget was an endless mystery. But now she seemed to be no different than any other woman, and it was *his* fault. She was far more beautiful, of course, but the fire within her was nowhere to be seen. She'd lost that spark, all because of him and his silly wager with Graham.

And as that realization hit him, he had a terrible thought. If Bridget had been changed in such a way, what if all the other women he'd known in his life, the ones he'd thought boring and inspiring had also been... changed. Perhaps nearly every woman in high society was forced to give up their dreams and desires and play the part of obedient, subservient daughters, sisters or wives. All of them had their uniqueness erased by society's expectations.

Dear god... If that was the case, he was a damned cad forever thinking of them the way he had. His own bloody hubris could very well have made him just as bad as any other man when he could have been encouraging his female acquaintances to come out of the shells society forced them to hide in.

Trystan snuck a glance at Bridget who sat quietly in the coach, her gaze a thousand miles away, and he made a vow in that moment to not judge any woman again the way he used to.

When they arrived at Lady Tremaine's, they removed their cloaks and Trystan led her with pride toward the ballroom. The master of ceremonies was waiting for them. As they stood in the line to be introduced, a tall, fair-haired man walked past them. Bridget sucked in a breath and froze, her face draining of color.

"What is it?" he asked her.

"That man. The handsome one with pale blonde hair. He has stopped at my father's tavern several times. I've spoken to him when I've served him and he was always very observant, not like the other men who came into the tavern for a drink. He might recognize me." She tried to slide her arm free, but Trystan placed a hand on hers, and gave her fingers a light, supportive squeeze.

"Just a moment, my dear," Trystan said. "He will not recognize you. Even I do not. Your transformation has left no doubt in the minds of those who know you that you are a lady, like all the others in this room. It is simply a fact now. That creature you once were in Penzance is gone. He cannot possibly guess about your past."

Trystan studied this man who was a threat to his

wager and silently cursed. He knew the fellow. They ran in similar circles and had been schoolmates as boys.

And then, as if the charming devil had heard his name called, the man turned and spotted Trystan. He shot Trystan a sardonic look before his gaze settled on Bridget. Curiosity blossomed on the man's face.

The master of ceremonies waved Trystan and Bridget forward, and they took their place as their names were announced.

"Lord Zennor and Miss Bridget Ringgold."

"Chin up, little cat. You own the world tonight," he said in a whisper and she lifted her chin higher, as serene as any duchess.

Trystan escorted Bridget to Lady Tremaine, where Bridget was greeted by the hostess. Lady Tremaine was a fine woman in her early forties, a clever yet compassionate widow.

He and Bridget performed the niceties of small talk with Lady Tremaine before she began summoning men to sign Bridget's dance card. She informed those who gathered that Bridget was the ward of Trystan's cousin from Yorkshire.

And of course, the last man in line was the man he and Bridget had wanted most to avoid. The man flashed that smile of his at Bridget. It was a smile that broke hearts all over London.

"Trystan, I must beg an introduction to your charming cousin's ward."

"Bridget, this is Mr. Rafe Lennox."

"It's lovely to meet you, Mr. Lennox," Bridget said.

Rafe bowed and kissed Bridget's gloved hand.

"The pleasure is all mine, I assure you," he said. "May I claim a dance?"

Bridget didn't say no, because she couldn't. A *lady* never refused to dance unless she was unfamiliar with the steps and therefore might embarrass her partner. It was one of the lessons that had been drilled into her over and over.

"Of course. It seems I have a couple of spots left." She lifted her card up and Rafe produced a small pencil, writing his name down for one of the dances.

"Until then, Miss Ringgold," Rafe Lennox promised.

Bridget nodded. Once he left, she let out a small and audible sigh of relief.

"As I said, he did not recognize you."

"He might if we spend more time together. Mr. Lennox was not shy to talk around me, and often asked questions about the goings-on around Penzance."

"All you have to do is survive one dance with him." Trystan put his name down on her card for the final dance of the night. "Here comes Kent. Stay with him for a moment while I bring you something to drink."

Trystan headed for the refreshment table to collect

glasses of arrack punch. As he walked through the crowds, he heard dozens of people whispering questions as to who the mystery beauty was who had been brought to the ball.

Trystan couldn't help but smile to himself in satisfaction.

❦

BRIDGET CLUTCHED HER CLOSED FAN WITH A trembling hand as she stared at Rafe Lennox's back. He was all the way across the room, engaged in conversation and not paying any attention to her. But she was still terrified that he might recognize her. He had visited the tavern frequently in the last two years, and she'd always served him. Most men of his rank did not ever look at the boys serving them their ale, but he had. His blue eyes could see anything and most likely saw everything. How on earth could she fool him? He would realize who she was, and there was a chance he would tell Lady Tremaine just who she really was. She wasn't entirely certain he would tell Lady Tremaine, but the possibility frightened her enough to worry about it.

The scandal would be the end of whatever hope she had for a better future, and Trystan would be drawn into a scandal when he came to her defense. And he would come to her defense, she knew that. Somehow, in the last month, the arrogant nobleman had come to care for her, though not nearly so much as she had come to care for him. But he cared enough that he wouldn't want to see her embarrassed or publicly humiliated.

Kent stayed by her side while Trystan fetched her a glass of punch, but the dancing began as he was on his way back. She now had to face the first gentleman on her card, who came over and claimed her for his dance. He was a handsome man with kind eyes and he spoke of his home, a place called Falconridge. She enjoyed learning about his home and he, in turn, asked her about her home. She had to keep her answers vague. Luckily, she knew a bit about Yorkshire thanks to Trystan's lessons on the subject.

She managed to relax a little while she danced with Lord Falconridge, conversing well with the man. And then she was returned to Trystan and Kent, and gratefully accepted her punch.

This continued with the others one by one, and with each dance, the facade she kept up required less effort and felt more natural. By the time the seventh dance ended, Graham came to claim her for his dance and carried with him unexpected news.

"Try not to panic," Graham said softly once they were a safe distance from the other couples. "But everyone here tonight is most curious about you."

"Why?" Bridget fought to keep panic showing on her face or in her voice. "Are they suspicious?"

"Not at all. They believe you are from the north, a part of the country that most of London thinks is cold, dreary and, frankly, a bit barbarous. But you come in here looking absolutely stunning, and it has them asking questions. You do know that you look singularly beautiful tonight, don't you? Every man in the room wishes to know who you are. And every woman is eyeing you with envy. They wish to know your entire life story. You see the potential for disaster, do you not?"

She peeped at the room around them, noting how many people were indeed looking at her.

"Oh dear, what should I do?"

"Three weeks ago I wouldn't have given you any advice, seeing as I very much would like to own Trystan's lodge in Scotland, but I've grown rather fond of you and have no desire to see you embarrassed. Surprising, isn't it?" He chuckled. "And because of that dreaded weakness, I will give you my advice."

He paused before continuing. The dance was ending, but she didn't dare rush him.

"My advice... is that you're doing fine. Not even Rafe Lennox will suspect a thing, because you *are* a lady, Bridget. No one could believe anything otherwise."

He winked at her and when the dance ended, she

spun to face the very man who had caused her so much concern tonight.

Rafe gave her a leonine smile as he offered her his hand.

"I believe I'm next?" He closed his fingers around hers and she was led back out for the next dance. The two faced each other across the line of dancers, and he bowed to her as the music began. This particular dance kept them apart for half of the time and back in each other's arms for the other half.

"Miss Ringgold, I must confess, I had the strangest feeling we've met before. We have, haven't we?"

Bridget's heart pounded hard, but she kept calm. She was a lady. Nothing could ruffle her if she didn't let it. They were separated for a moment by a pair of dancers, then came back together.

"No, I'm sorry, but we haven't met until tonight."

"Really? Perhaps you remind me of someone then. But who?" His bemused smile didn't ease her fears. "Everyone is just as curious as I am. You've created quite the stir tonight."

They parted once again as they circled around another group of dancers before coming back together.

"I could swear that we've met, though," he persisted. She answered his searching look with a polite smile.

"I would have remembered, Mr. Lennox. You have quite the presence." She gave him a flirtatious smile.

He grinned at her, sensing she was up to something. "I rather like you, Miss Ringgold. I'm sure that I shan't be the only man interested in you."

As the dance finally ended, he bowed over her hand and suddenly smiled. "I remember now..."

It took every ounce of her will not to flinch and pull away.

"Remember what, Mr. Lennox?" she asked.

"You remind me of a friend of my brother's. Anna Maria Zelensky. The Princess of Ruritania. Have you met her?"

"No, I'm afraid I haven't had the pleasure."

"Pity. I think you and Anna would like each other. She was in London last fall, and now she's in Scotland with her husband. He's a friend of mine, Aiden Kincade."

None of those names meant anything to her, and she worried that he noticed her lack of reaction.

"She is a quiet beauty, but there is a fire in her, a ferocity of spirit that I sense you have as well. You may be from Yorkshire, but you could pass for a princess. It was a pleasure dancing with you, Miss Ringgold."

"And you, Mr. Lennox." She beamed at him as she realized she had passed the ultimate test, one she never could have prepared for in advance.

Once Rafe left, she had a chance to drink another

glass of punch before Trystan claimed her for the final waltz.

"The room was abuzz with talk," he said as he held her in his arms.

"Oh? About what?" She feigned innocence, even though she knew what he was referring to.

"Rafe is telling everyone that you remind him of Princess Anna of Ruritania. And gossip being what it is, more than one person now suspects you are a princess in disguise. That means you've done it. Now be at ease, little cat, and waltz with me. I'm quite tired of seeing other men having you in their arms when I've waited nearly three hours for this pleasure."

Trystan smiled at her and she felt rather dizzy. She'd waited all night for this waltz too. As they began to dance, an unexpected relief swept through her like a surging wave over the shores of Zennor.

"We won the wager," she whispered in excitement.

"We did." He grinned back at her. "And now you will sleep tonight and dream of a fresh start," he continued.

Yes, she would dream of it, but that dream held a note of bitterness, because that future wouldn't have him in it. Tonight was perhaps the last time she would ever dance with him. Bridget was resolved to enjoy herself as much as possible, and she tried to savor her victory. But all too soon, that perfect dance with her perfect partner came to an end.

"Are you ready to go home?" he asked.

She was weary now that her final test was over at last. She could sleep for a week. "Yes, take me home, Trystan."

They found Kent and Graham near the doors leading out of the ballroom. Their party bid good night to Lady Tremaine, who insisted that they must bring this most charming girl back to call upon her soon. With the blushed murmur that she would be delighted too, Bridget and her three escorts departed and headed home.

When they arrived at Trystan's townhouse, his London butler, Mr. Fydell greeted them. Kent gave the butler the good news.

"Trys has done it. He's won the wager!"

"Yes, yes, all praise Trystan," Graham grumbled. but he was smiling as he pretended to be annoyed.

"Well done, my lord," Mr. Fydell exclaimed to his master.

Bridget couldn't believe it. It had happened again. She slid out of her coat and was completely ignored by the gentlemen as she walked upstairs to her bedchamber. As she reached the door, she realized that the men were celebrating downstairs and no one had asked her to join in. It was just like the night they had dined at Lady Helena's dinner party.

She entered her room and found Marvella waiting up

for her. Marvella helped her undress for the night and Bridget collected her jewelry, putting the diamonds into a small velvet case. Something about the act of putting away such shining beauty, to be stored away until it was needed next, finally set her off.

Gripping the case, and wearing nothing but her chemise and housecoat with slippers, she stormed down to the billiard room where the three men were drinking brandy and laughing about their success at fooling one of London's most clever rakehells.

"Little cat, what the devil are you doing up? Go to bed, you silly creature." Trystan waved her off before he took a long drink of his brandy.

She tamped down the building rage inside her. "These are for you. I assume they should be returned if I leave tomorrow morning." She left the diamond box upon the green baize surface of the billiard table and walked out of the room, leaving a thunderous silence behind her.

She was halfway up the stairs when she heard Trystan shout her name, but she didn't stop until he caught her at the top of the staircase.

"Why, you ungrateful creature," he said, as he tried to push the diamonds back at her.

"I am not ungrateful. I am *tired*." She let the box fall to the floor between them and headed for her bedchamber.

"Bridget, come back at once. We are not done talking."

She sped up and had just reached her room when he joined her at the open door. The maid blinked in surprise at the pair of them as she pulled the covers back on the bed.

"Please leave us, Marvella," Trystan ordered, his tone as hard as the diamonds he held in his palm.

"Miss?" Marvella asked Bridget with concern.

"Go on to bed. I'll be fine," she reassured Marvella.

Marvella swallowed hard and then nodded before she left. When the door clicked shut behind them, Bridget felt her fury clash with Trystan's in a blinding storm, but neither of them moved.

"These diamonds were a gift," he said, his tone dangerously soft. "You were the most brilliant and beautiful woman at the ball tonight, and we have spent what I thought was a most agreeable time together. You earned the diamonds. You should keep them."

"Earned?" The word made her think of a future spent lying on her back. "How *dare* you —?" She raised her palm to strike him. He caught her wrist, preventing it.

"I didn't mean it like that, and you bloody well know it." He continued to hold her arm and stepped closer. "Keep the diamonds. I have no use for them."

"I don't wish to keep anything that you paid for, not any longer. I will only take what I brought with me—"

"Now you are being a fool."

"Fool?"

"Yes, a fool. If you left with only what you'd brought, all that you'd have are those boy togs to wear," he growled. "We had an agreement, an understanding. Everything you have been given has been earned, not some act of charity to turn your nose up at. Only a fool would toss all that away because they're upset with me. Never mind the fact that I don't even know *why* you are upset. Now go to bed. You'll feel better tomorrow. Tomorrow we can settle the accounts and you can move into a quaint little cottage that I have ready for you. It will—"

"I don't want to go to any *bloody* cottage. Leave me alone!" she snarled. His calm, callous talk of her leaving drove her to a new level of pain, and she started to cry despite her deepest not to do so. "*Please...* just leave me alone."

But he didn't. He pulled her into his arms, holding her tight, his lips pressing against her ear.

"There, there, little cat." He soothed. "I didn't mean to upset you. *I'm* the fool. You did wonderful tonight and you deserve a night sky full of diamonds," he said, and his tenderness somehow made how she felt worse and her crying grew louder. "Hush now, or I'll have to kiss you to make you feel better."

When she couldn't stop weeping, he lifted her face

up and his lips found hers. The simple connection left her feeling grounded, like a tree sinking roots into soil so deep that no storm could ever tear it away from that bit of land it stood upon. This man had become her soil, the earth that she could dig into safely, to grow and thrive through the mightiest of storms.

His mouth moved tenderly over hers, and she slid her arms up over his shoulders to hold onto him. A soft thud at her feet made her think only dimly of the diamonds that he must have dropped, but she cared only for Trystan's kiss.

He walked her backward until she was up against one of the bedposts. Then he slid her housecoat off her shoulders, and she stepped free of her slippers.

"Stay," he said to her before he left her briefly to retrieve one of her extra hair ribbons from her vanity table. When he came back, he stood in silent question, holding up the ribbon, and she answered with a desperate little sound that made him kiss her again. She didn't know what he meant to do, but she trusted him. He pressed her back against the bedpost again, then bound her wrists with the ribbon and lifted them above her head before he tied the rest of the ribbon to the post. She was helpless and her body throbbed almost painfully with need.

"You're so beautiful," Trystan murmured as he smoothed his palms down her arms from her wrists to her shoulders. She trembled, feeling vulnerable as he gazed at her, a wolfish gleam in his eyes.

"I feared I'd lost that brazen part of you that burns with fire, but here it is. I found it and I dare not lose you again."

He loved that part of her? The part that had frustrated him so often? Something about that made her heart blossom with warmth and left her dizzy with joy.

He unfastened the ribbons of her chemise above her breasts and then, gripping the material in his hands, he wrenched it apart, ripping it clear down to her upper belly. She always found her bodily curves bothersome, but as he gazed at her, she finally welcomed the fullness of her breasts.

He cupped one in his hand and brushed his thumb over her nipple, then lightly pinched it. She groaned as a searing heat shot straight to her womb. He bent his head to her other breast and took her nipple between his lips. The tug on her sensitive peak sent a flood of wet heat between her thighs. She clenched them together, trying to erase a throbbing that only deepened. He moved his mouth to her other breast, sucking until she was impossibly wet. He stood before her still fully clothed while she was nearly naked and tied to the bed. Why did that make her so feel so wild and excited?

Trystan removed his coat and unfastened his neck cloth, draping them both over the nearest chair. Then he folded the sleeves of his shirt past his elbows to expose his arms as he returned to her. He leaned in, kissing her lips while he teased her nipples with his fingers. Then he fisted his hand in her hair and held her head still as he delved deeper into her mouth, his tongue lightly thrusting into her mouth as his other hand slid up her thigh until it reached the folds of her sex. He didn't tease her this time. He simply thrust his fingers in, ruthlessly penetrating her where she craved it most.

"Tell me now if you want to stop..." he warned as he lifted his head from hers. His fingers were still deep inside her and her channel throbbed around them. Bridget lifted her hips, trying to push the fingers deeper.

"Tell me yes or no, Bridget. Yes, and I will claim your body right here, right now. No, and I shall release you and tuck you into bed and let you sleep."

She knew what her answer was, knew it, and had no hesitation. No matter what happened after, she would have this moment to remember.

"Yes... Trystan... yes," she begged. "Teach me this..." She needed him to teach her to make love more than she needed anything else in her life.

His whiskey-brown eyes darkened and he curled two fingers inside her, hitting a secret spot within her that made her eyes roll back in her head. He stroked that place until she was quaking with desire. Then he withdrew his hand and knelt at her feet. He ripped the rest of her chemise open and bared her body fully to his gaze. He kissed her belly, then her abdomen, then he lifted one of her legs and rested it on his shoulder as he opened her to him.

"Trystan, what are you do—" She ended her question on a shriek as his mouth settled on the top of her mound and he sucked.

"Oh no..." she moaned as he began to lick her folds. She'd never imagined a man could do that down there, and it felt *unbelievably strange and wonderful.*

His hands cupped her bottom from behind and he spanked her twice, the little smacks only making her wetter. His tongue slid into her and she begged for him to take her, to give her what she needed, whatever it was. He only chuckled against her burning flesh before he continued to lick her.

Then she came apart in an explosion like she had at the old Saxon ruins, bursting open and then being knitted back together piece by piece. She sagged limply against the bedpost, but he stood up and shrugged off his waistcoat and then removed his boots and opened his trousers. His thick cock sprang free, jutting toward her, massive and daunting, but she had no energy to speak, to ask if he would even fit inside her.

Trystan lifted Bridget up against the bedpost, her legs widening around him as he pinned her against the wood. Then he guided himself into her and thrust deep, hard, the pain of his entry intense but brief before he sank too deep for her not to feel the rest of him filling and stretching her. His forehead touched hers as he held himself very still within her, their breath mingling.

"Does it still hurt?" he asked as if he was fighting a battle to hold still.

"N—no, not much," she replied in a whisper.

"Good, because now I'm going to make love to you, little cat. Do you understand? You will be a toy for my pleasure. I will use you for my desires and I will make you almost perish with your own pleasure."

The thought of Trystan using her like that... like a toy, yet seeing to her own pleasure... made her desperate to climax all over again. She squirmed between him and the bedpost, trying to get closer.

He chuckled, the sound dark and delicious as he withdrew and rocked back into her. His eyes studied her face, for what she wasn't sure, but he seemed satisfied before he deepened his next thrust and quickened his pace. His hips began to buck against her over and over, his cock surging deep into her as her body shook with the force of it. It felt *glorious.*

The power of their union made her feel wild and unfettered with passion despite her bound wrists. It was the most exquisite thing she'd ever known. She could moan and claw like the hellcat she was. She could embrace the battle of their union and his conquering of her body because it was her choice to surrender to this wild part of herself. There was no shame, only mutual respect for their pleasure.

He rammed deeper into her, his kisses tasted of hunger, and it seemed to go on forever, this intense duel of kisses and frenzied mating. When his mouth finally broke apart from hers, he turned his face toward her neck, biting her shoulder as his hands gripped her buttocks and clenched hard. He hammered her over and over, and when the dam finally burst she couldn't even scream. She was overwhelmed with the orgasm that roared through her. Spots danced across her vision and she went limp again. Trystan pounded against her for another few strokes before he shouted her name. Something hot filled her and she clenched her thighs tight against his hips, holding him to her, feeling the need now more than ever to stay connected to this man.

Trystan panted against her ear and then lightly kissed her cheek. For a long moment, neither of them said a word as he embraced her with impossible tenderness. Then he carefully let her legs drop from his hips and unfastened the ribbon from the bed post, freeing her arms. She rubbed her wrists, unconcerned with the faint red marks left on her skin. When he eased out of her body, she feared that he would leave her to sleep, but instead he went to wet a cloth in the basin on the washstand and came back to her. He cleaned between her thighs. She was too tired to be embarrassed at the bit of blood she saw him wipe away. She shrugged off the rest of her ripped chemise and pressed her fist against her mouth, stifling a yawn. Trystan pulled her into his arms and kissed her sweetly. If she hadn't been so tired, she might have cried again.

"In bed now, if you please." He gave her bottom another light spank and then nudged her toward the bed. She collapsed onto it, fully naked, and lay on her stomach. She watched him clean himself with the cloth, and he removed his trousers and stockings. When he came back to the bed, he was fully naked.

"Move over, hellion. I plan to sleep and I wish to hold you."

With a sigh of contentment, she slid over and let him get beneath the covers before she joined him, and they cuddled in his embrace.

"Tomorrow we must talk. But tonight... tonight..." He didn't finish.

Bridget was glad. She didn't want to know what he would have said.

Tomorrow would be here soon enough, and she would face her choices then. For now, she would pretend that tomorrow wasn't ever going to come and that she would stay here with Trystan in bed forever... happy and free.

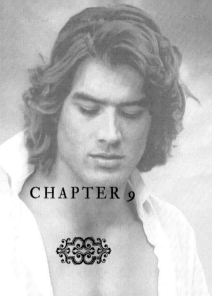

CHAPTER 9

Trystan had made a terrible mistake last night. He felt the weight of that error as he finished writing his letter to Bridget. It reminded her in no uncertain terms that she had no future with him. He'd had his old seaside cottage made ready for her in the past week. He'd decided to give it to her free and clear—that way, she need not worry about finding a place on her own.

In the letter, he'd explained about the cottage and how she should be ready to leave for it soon. Then, if she wished to find employment somewhere, he'd write her a letter of recommendation that was bound to assure her of getting whatever position she wished. Trystan promised he would send along her wardrobe, her new horse and some staff to take care of her and the property. It was his desire to reward her for her part in the wager and that she need not worry about seeing him again. She was free to do as she wished now. But why did even thinking about her being gone from his life cast a gray, listless pall over his future?

He folded the letter and crept back into Bridget's bedchamber. To his relief, she was still asleep. He placed the paper on the pillow beside her and then, on an impulse, he took the bloom of a rose from a nearby vase and placed it on top of the letter. Bridget sighed softly and turned in her sleep, her hand sliding across the bed where he had lain. He would have given anything to crawl back beneath the covers with her. But if he didn't walk away now, he might never manage it.

"Goodbye, little cat," he whispered. Then he saw one last diamond star cluster still pinned into the coils of her hair. It winked in the sunlight, reminding him of every incredible moment they shared last night, from dancing at the ball to making love and feeling truly free with her.

He suddenly found it hard to swallow as he backed out of the bedchamber and closed the door. He turned around and came face to face with Marvella, who had a stack of fresh linens in her arms. Her eyes widened a little at the sight of him slipping out of Bridget's bedchamber.

"Er... good morning, Marvella," he said rather quickly. Then he fled downstairs, retrieved his coat and hat, and told his butler he was bound for his club. Bridget would read the letter soon enough and leave. That would be the end of it.

THE CONVERSATION TRYSTAN HAD PROMISED TO share with her the morning following the ball never came. When Bridget woke up, she found the bed empty and a letter with a lovely, deep red rose laying on top of the pillow where his head had rested the night before.

With a trembling hand, she cupped the rose in her hands and brought it up to her nose to take in its scent. Then she laid it down and opened the letter.

> Bridget,
> I made a mistake bedding you last night. No, hellcat, I do not regret the second of our time together. I only regret that I cannot give you more than one. My mistake was caring too much for you despite not being able to give you what you deserve. A life as a countess would not make you happy. You would face hardship and judg-

ment at every turn once the truth was known, and I could not bear to watch you struggle and suffer.

I have left a packet for you with Mr. Fydell. It contains the deed to the cottage where I wish you to live, and I have told Fydell that Marvella may go with you and still receive her same wages. The cottage will have a cook, a butler and a few other servants to help you. It has ten bedrooms and should give you plenty of room to bloom like any flower will with space and sunlight.

I know you must be furious with me, but rest assured that if any consequences come from our night together, I will provide you all that you need to live and keep yourself and our child healthy and happy. Please know that you have given me something to remember. I shall hold our night in my heart forever.

Yours,
Trystan

SHE STARED AT THE LETTER, SO MUCH OF IT overwhelming to her. But the thing that kept drawing her focus over and over was... *the consequences of their night*. She drew in a shaky breath and placed a hand to her belly. Was a child growing within her? She knew next to nothing of such womanly matters.

Despite her years of rough living, she was in many ways far too innocent, yet *he* had known the risks last night. She could have slapped him for that, if nothing else. If she was with child, she would *make* him know the child. She would not let their baby grow up without knowing its father. He would face that situation whether he liked it or not.

Bridget sat in bed a long while, staring at the letter until she felt she had memorized it. Marvella quietly tidied up the room, leaving Bridget to her thoughts until finally she rose from her bed.

"Are you all right, Miss?" Marvella asked.

"Yes... no. I honestly don't know. Trystan has given me a cottage to live in, and he said he would let you come with me and still pay your wages. Do you wish to come?" She desperately hoped Marvella would agree. The lady's maid had become her friend in the last month they had been together.

"I would be happy to," Marvella came over and put an arm around Bridget in a hug. "Why don't I bring you breakfast?"

"Thank you."

Bridget got dressed after a small meal, then had a discussion with Mr. Fydell about the documents to the cottage. With some guidance from him, she planned to have things packed and one of Trystan's travel coaches made ready to leave that afternoon.

She was finishing up her goodbyes to the London townhouse staff when Lord Kent arrived. He and Graham, she had learned, had gone to their own London townhouses after she had interrupted the brandy celebration in the billiard room the previous evening.

Kent removed his hat and waited in the entryway with her. The servants slipped away to give them privacy.

"You're leaving?" he asked, his gentle eyes full of concern.

"Yes, Trystan has told me to retire to his cottage by the sea, but I have other things to do and I thought it best I leave straightaway to do them."

"Other things?" Kent smiled, but the expression held a hint of sorrow. "Dare I ask what they are?"

She smiled back at him. "Oh... I think I have a few more adventures to stir up before I let Trystan make an old spinster of me. Is it all right that I take Beau with me?"

"Of course. He is my gift to you." Kent rubbed his thumb over the silver handle of his cane. "Would you like some company on these adventures? I could go with you."

She reached up and placed her palm on his cheek. "You have always treated me like a lady, Lord Kent. You cannot know what that means. But now I need to explore the world on my own and learn what this new version of myself is capable of. But you can do something for me."

"Name it."

"Take care of Trystan. I fear that he will be reckless. Do not let him get hurt."

Kent held out a hand to her and she placed her palm in his.

"Until we have the fortune of meeting again, Bridget."

"Phillip," she replied, feeling almost shy now at using his given name. She supposed she really was a lady. Whatever unruly creature she had once been, with crude language and rude manners, she was changed. There was a part of her that grieved the loss of her old self, and she'd once feared that Trystan's lessons had left her useless, but they hadn't. She would still be a lady, but she would set her own rules for living. She wouldn't play the role of a quiet little spinster in a cottage by the sea even if it did have ten rooms and sounded more like a palace. She would visit it soon, but she wasn't about to confine her existence there, Trystan's wishes be damned.

TWO MONTHS LATER...

Trystan stared at Mr. Chavenage. "What the devil do you mean, she never arrived at the cottage?"

His butler squared his shoulders, keeping calm in the face of Trystan's fury. It was one of the reasons he paid Mr. Chavenage so well. The man handled Trystan's mercurial moods with grace.

"Mr. Gaythan, your butler at the cottage, wrote to me this morning when I inquired about Miss Ringgold staying there. He said she never arrived."

"And why am I only hearing about this *now?*"

"She wrote to him shortly after the staff arrived, explaining she would come at some point before the summer ended and not to worry about her until she arrived."

"Not to worry?" Trystan shredded the nearest letter in front of him to pieces. Thankfully, it was only a missive from Graham, which he had already read before his butler had come into the study.

"Why didn't you inquire about her sooner, Chavenage?"

His butler gave him a rather frustrated look. "Well, given how close the cottage is, I rather thought *you* would have visited her yourself, my lord."

Well, damnation, the man has a point there, Trystan silently admitted.

He had given Bridget that cottage to keep her close, but he never planned to *visit* her. That would have been highly improper as well as dangerous to his heart.

"Where the devil is the girl if she hasn't been there at the cottage?" he asked, not exactly expecting Mr. Chavenage to answer him.

"I haven't the faintest idea, my lord. She has sent *these*, however, to Mrs. Story." The butler proffered several short letters. They bore locations from Edinburgh to Brighton Beach.

"She sent these?" He studied Bridget's handwriting in the brief stories she'd written to the housekeeper.

"Apparently. Mrs. Story didn't know the girl was not supposed to be out exploring, as it were, so she didn't think to mention she'd been receiving the letters until this morning when I discussed all this with her."

"*Exploring*," Trystan muttered as he examined the letters. She certainly had been, if the quickly jotted stories were true. She'd been swimming at Brighton Beach, touring museums and monuments in Scotland. She'd even sailed along the south of England in a cutter ship and toured the Isle of Skye in the north of Scotland. She was learning to speak French from Marvella, who had learned to speak the language years ago. The two girls planned to visit France at some point. He'd given Bridget a good deal of money when he'd created an account for her through a bank that a friend of his owned, and he hadn't bothered to check on what she'd done with the money. Clearly she'd gone on adventures with it. And rather than staying furious... he felt intrigued and oddly amused.

Trystan realized he was actually smiling. The little hellion had proved him wrong. He thought he had molded her into a swan like all the other women in London. But he hadn't. She'd *always* been a swan; he'd merely shown her she could fly. He felt a sudden pang of regret that he was not with her. He would have loved to see her in a bathing costume as she collected shells and felt the sea caress her skin. He would have laughed with her as he listened to her stories while they rode through the Highlands on Beau's back.

"My little cat is *living*," he said, his throat oddly tight.

"My lord?"

"Er... return these to Mrs. Story. Tell her I want to know the *moment* she receives another. I might be able to find Bridget's location, or at the least catch her trail." He tapped his stack of unopened letters thoughtfully with his finger. "I think I shall go see my great aunt this afternoon. Please have my horse saddled."

His butler left him alone, and he took a moment to collect the shredded remnants of Graham's letter. After he had won the wager, Graham had immediately offered his racing curricle and his team of horses as payment, but when Trystan had given it a few days thought, he declined to accept it. Graham had insisted on the trade being made, but Trystan had finally met him for drinks at their club and explained why he couldn't accept. Graham had helped Bridget almost as much as Trystan and Kent had in her preparations, and it was not fair to take the winnings when the man had gone out of his way to help Trystan win.

In the end, Graham accepted this and they drank whiskey in companionable silence by the fire, but after a moment his friend smiled wistfully and said he wished Bridget was there with them. Her absence felt so strange after she'd been so constantly present for over a month.

Graham was right. He had grown accustomed to the girl. For all the time they had spent in study and prac-tice, there had been so much more that had happened— all of which he now fondly remembered. She would cuddle up in the chair opposite him by the fire and read a book while he read his own. Graham and Kent would play chess, and sometimes the four of them would play whist or faro. He couldn't count the times in the last two months that he'd wandered the halls of his home in Zennor and chased the ghosts of her memory. As much as he wished it, his memories could not resurrect her spirit.

She had settled right into his life as if she'd always been a vital piece of it. He'd never realized that until now, how she'd become crucial to his day. He'd *enjoyed* living with her under his roof. Such a curious thing, really. But what could he do? He couldn't marry the girl, couldn't put her through what his mother had endured. He couldn't risk having her spirit broken. She should be living her own life, just as she was doing now.

An hour later, he rode toward Lady Helena's home and was shown inside by his great aunt's butler. Helena was in the conservatory cutting roses. Her spectacles were perched on her nose and the light purple gown she wore was shielded by an apron dotted with soil stains. She greeted him with a hug and a kiss on his cheek.

"What is my favorite nephew doing here?" she asked as she cut another rose and tucked it in a vase on a nearby table.

"Well, I don't honestly know." He supposed he'd come because he'd needed to talk with someone who loved and cared about him, yet he also needed someone who would be honest.

Lady Helena chuckled. "Well, you do look lost," his aunt said. "And where's my darling Bridget?" she asked.

"Bridget?" he echoed.

"Yes, she always comes to see me when you do." Lady Helena continued cutting roses.

That was certainly true; he'd taken to visiting his

aunt twice a week in the last month and Bridget had adored coming along. She and Helena had gotten along famously, and the sight of their heads bent together in discussion always made his chest tighten and flood with warmth.

"Oh... she's gone." He had a sudden need to unburden himself to his great aunt.

"Gone?" Helena repeated the word with clear fear that something had befallen Bridget.

"She's left...I mean. The wager is over and she's gone out on her own, just as we'd always planned." It was the truth, but why did saying those words leave such a terrible, hollow ache in his chest? By leaving, she'd taken not only herself but part of his own soul away, and all he had were memories that simply weren't enough. He'd been lying to himself for weeks now, saying he didn't care that she was gone. But he bloody well cared.

"Tell me everything, dear boy."

She handed him a pair of shears, and he took up work beside her, cutting roses. He'd always liked such a task. His mother had taught him well how to attend to growing things. As they cut roses side-by-side, Trystan told Helena all that had happened at the ball, how Bridget had come off as regal as a princess and how she fooled everyone, even the cunning Rafe Lennox who had met her at that old tavern several times. When she was finally done, she removed her gloves and set her shears down.

"So now my little cat has wandered off, and I don't know where she is, or even if she is safe. It has me deuced worried because—"

"You love her," his aunt finished.

"I cannot—"

"Do not lie to me, Trystan. Nor should you lie to yourself. I'm far too old and yet my ears, as deaf as they are sometimes, still cannot abide to hear a lie about love." She removed the gardening apron from her dress and set it on the table, then fixed him with a motherly stare.

"Aunt Helena, I—"

"What is the harm in admitting you love Bridget? Will a bolt of lightning strike you down?"

"I rather feel like it might," he grumbled. "Admitting something like that... It's, well, it's not done, is it? Only fools fall in love. I can't marry for love and I have no desire to marry for advantage either, so where does that leave me?"

"Rather *alone*, I should say," Helena said quite bluntly. "While there's certainly nothing wrong with being alone —I've quite enjoyed my solitude—you on the other hand would be a damned fool for walking away from the love of your life. And what's wrong with marrying for love? Your father did."

"And look at what happened to him." Trystan set his shears down on the table a little too forcefully. His great aunt's eyes narrowed behind her spectacles.

"What happened is that your parents were very happy. They loved each other and had a wonderful son."

"But it didn't *end* happily," he reminded her. That old pain of loss dug its claws into him again. "Mother was shunned by everyone in father's social circles."

Helena nodded sadly. "Because she was a Romani. Yes, I am aware."

"She was treated as an outcast, and it drove her to an early grave. I suffered enough as a boy, being teased about my gypsy blood. But now I'm grown, and it doesn't bother me one bit what others say. But father... He never was the same after losing mother." He had *never* spoken so openly in his life about something so painful, but now that he'd started, he couldn't seem to stop.

"Don't you see? The truth about Bridget would come out, and then she would face the same situation as my mother. I would marry her in an instant but... but I can't stand by and watch her break the way my mother did. Yes, she fooled everyone at Lady Tremaine's ball, but that facade cannot be maintained forever. She would be laughed at, ridiculed, *destroyed*. I couldn't bear to witness that."

Helena stared at him. "Have you bothered to talk to

Bridget about your true feelings? She's not nearly so much like your mother as you think."

"Of course I haven't. I didn't want her to think there was a chance of marriage when there isn't."

"Trystan, dear," she said more gently. "Your mother was a wild and carefree creature, the same as Bridget, but she was also a delicate flower. Your father knew that when he married her. He took the risk of sharing his life with her, and so did she. But Bridget is not the same. That young woman has had to fight to survive her entire life. She's thrived in situations when others barely hang on. She's *not* a delicate flower. She's an oak with deep roots. She wouldn't let anyone push her out, not like your mother. Besides, if anyone dared give her the cut direct, I imagine that a wide circle of men and women who are fiercely loyal to you would do the same to those who would dare cut your wife out of society. She has protectors—she has *you*—but most importantly, she has *herself*. A strong woman cares not for the opinions of others, but only her opinion of herself. That is where confidence comes from, and when someone carries confidence as a shield, the barbs and arrows of the insecure and jealous find no weak spots to strike."

Trystan stared in awe at his great aunt. She was right, and he had been too afraid to admit it because he was not ready himself to admit he had fallen in love.

"Well then, what are your plans, dear boy? You

cannot stand here pruning roses forever, no matter how much I may enjoy your company."

"Er... no, I suppose not." He stared hopelessly down at the pair of sheers he had placed on the potting bench.

"Don't just stand there. Instead of running away from her, go after her." Helena threw a gardening glove at his face. It smacked him, and he just managed to catch it before it fell to the ground.

"I have no idea where she is. She could be anywhere in England. And what if she doesn't want me? What if she doesn't need me?"

"Do you want her to need you?" Helena asked.

He was silent a long moment. "I only want her to love me...but I've been so terribly commanding towards her. What if she thinks I am commanding her to come home like some trained spaniel?"

At this his aunt laughed merrily. "Heavens, where do you come up with such nonsense? Bridget isn't a spaniel and you know it. That girl has a lovely bite to her, like any good wildcat. You never tame or control a creature like that. You feed it, care for it, love it and eventually one night, you'll find it's snuggled up in your arms, content as a kitten." She cut another rose and placed it in the vase, then stepped back to admire her work.

"Why did you never marry?" Trystan asked his aunt. He'd never given his aunt's solitary life much thought until now.

"Because I was like Bridget and there was only one man for me in all the world. He died while fighting the American colonists. When he never came home, I simply decided there was no one else who would ever take his place, and while I kept my heart open, I was right. He was a once in a lifetime kind of love." Her voice was soft, and full of an ancient heartache that Trystan was now feeling himself as he thought of Bridget somewhere far away, living a life without him because he'd failed to tell her he loved her.

"I'm sorry, Aunt Helena, I didn't know."

She turned to face him and reached out, her gloved hands giving his a gentle squeeze.

"She wants you, Trystan, trust an old woman when I say that I know what love looks like. She's only ever looked at you with love in her eyes, even when she's been upset with you. Isn't that the measure of love? To love through the anger and the pain when one must?"

Trystan found his throat unbearably tight as he tried to speak. "You aren't old," he said.

She laughed and cupped his cheek fondly, her eyes bright. "My bones might be, but the spirit is forever young," she patted his cheek once and then turned back to her pruning again.

"What should I do?" he asked.

Helena rolled her eyes as if the answer was obvious.

"Why don't you go home and sleep on it? I expect you'll find a clue sooner than you think."

"Yes, good idea," he mused thoughtfully. As he turned to leave, he saw a small wooden carving on the bench where he'd so thoughtlessly slammed his shears down. His aunt had her back turned to him as he picked up the wooden carving. It was the size of his hand and it depicted a man with a noble-looking face. The wood had been smoothed with diligent, loving care and he recognized the style just as much as he recognized his own face starting back at him from the carving. Bridget had been here... sometime recently... but when? He didn't ask his aunt; she wouldn't have told him. This was his quest, after all—to earn Bridget's love and trust again. He pocketed the small carving in his coat, then came back over to his aunt.

He kissed his great aunt's cheek before he left the conservatory, and she returned to her pruning. Rather than wait for the groom to bring his horse around, he decided to go out to the stable himself. As he entered the door, he halted the sight of the familiar chestnut horse munching on a pail of oats in one of the stalls.

"Beau?" He walked over to the beast and patted its neck, making sure his eyes were not deceiving him. "If you are here, your mistress must be close by, eh?" So Bridget had come here and perhaps she was still here. He gave the horse another pat before he called for a groom to saddle his horse. He needed to get home at once. He would set a plan in motion to catch his wayward little cat in a parson's mousetrap.

⚜

LADY HELENA WAITED UNTIL SHE WAS CERTAIN HER nephew was gone, then spoke to a distant corner of the conservatory, where several tall trees and plants blocked a private sitting area.

"You may come out now. He's gone."

Bridget peered around a bush. "You're certain?"

Helena chuckled. "Yes. How much were you able to hear?"

"Everything," Bridget admitted.

"And?" Helena picked up the vase of roses. Bridget rushed forward, taking the heavy object from her.

"And what?" Bridget followed Helena as they left the conservatory and walked toward the drawing room.

"You heard him, child. The man loves you. More importantly, he's *in* love with you."

Bridget set the vase down on a table by the window and looked out at the garden beyond the glass.

"Do you think he would marry me? If he wasn't so worried that I'd break?"

"I believe he would," Helena said. "Now he understands how strong you are. He was too blinded by his fear of the past to see it before, but he's thinking clearly now."

Helena sat down in a chair, her bones aching with the day's work in the conservatory, but she didn't mind. At her age, the aches reminded her that she had lived a long and good life, one that was far from over if she had any say in it. She wanted to see Trystan and Bridget give her a dozen great-grandnephews and great-grandnieces.

"Would you marry him if he asked you to?"

The young woman adjusted the roses in the vase, then winced as she was pricked by a thorn. Rather than cry out or fuss, she simply sucked at the wound before resuming her sorting. Helena smiled. *Definitely an oak tree, this one*, she thought.

"I would, if he truly meant it. I *won't* be an obligation to him, nor an ornament. I need him to want me, to want to be with me the way I want to be with him."

She fretted over the blooms a little longer, then sat down in a chair with a frustrated sigh.

"There's so much I want to do still, so much to see. What if he won't let me do those things?"

Helena chuckled. "I'd like to see him or anyone else try to stop you. He will either join you or not, and I think he'll join you. For a man of leisure, he likes to be busy. He can't sit still very long, just like you."

Bridget laughed. "We're certainly matched in that, aren't we?"

"Yes. Now come and help me plan my next dinner party." Helena distracted the girl from her worries and hid her smile. She was an excellent chess player. She would wait for Trystan to make his move, and then she would send the queen running into his arms.

CHAPTER 10

Bridget stared at the old run-down tavern at the edge of Penzance. It hadn't changed at all in the last three months since she had left it.

"Miss Bridget, what should I do while you're gone?" Marvella asked.

"Wait here for me in the coach. Do not go out. This part of the town is not reputable."

Her loyal maid nodded and squeezed Bridget's hand before she returned to the waiting coach and disappeared inside.

"Back again," Bridget sighed to herself.

Had it really only been three months? The life she'd lived here had felt like a century ago. She checked the little bonnet on her head and adjusted the large orange ribbon underneath her chin. Then she lifted the skirts of her fine walking dress and strode toward the tavern. She knew she painted a lovely picture in the sky-blue satin gown with puffed sleeves and orange flowers embroidered on her bodice. Men in the street eyed her with respect and appreciation.

She stepped inside, her vision momentarily dim as she adjusted to the light. A familiar figure stood by the bar, cleaning glasses with a dirty cloth and grumbling. When he lifted his head, she waited to see a spark of recognition in the man's eyes, but none came. Instead, her stepfather nearly tripped over himself to offer her a seat and food. The old Bridget would have laughed and called the man out for failing to recognize her, but now she cared nothing for the man who'd once been her only family left in the world.

"What can I get you, milady?" he asked.

"An ale, please," she said calmly, then surveyed the room and smiled. A man at a distant table sat with his back to her, in his hand a small wooden carving. His dark, wavy hair gleamed in the muted sunlight that came through the grimy windows that looked out on the street. Without another glance at her stepfather, she picked up the mug and walked toward the man at the distant table, stopping just behind him.

"Oi, what do you want to drink, fancy pants?" she demanded rudely in her old accent.

"Watch your tongue and bring me a mug of ale," the

man commanded as he set the wooden carving on the table.

She slammed the ale down beside his arm on the table, and it sloshed dangerously close to his hand. He caught her wrist in a flash and pulled her so that she landed with her bottom sitting in his lap. She steadied herself by placing her palms on his chest. The man wrapped his arms around her, holding her securely on his lap.

"Hello, darling," Trystan said, his gaze heated with a fire she had missed ever since she had left him. Then there was the way he'd called her darling. He'd never done that before, and it made her heart flutter like mad.

"Hello," she greeted with a hesitant smile. Both ignored the fact that she was in his lap in a very public place. "Why did you come back *here*?" She nodded at the tavern around them.

"To find *you*, of course."

"But I wasn't here—" She halted abruptly, not wanting to give away the fact that she had been hiding for the last week at Lady Helena's home. He picked up the carving from the table and held it up before her. It was the one she'd done of his face when she'd been staying at Helena's home for a few days. She'd wondered where she'd left it. He must have found it when he came to visit his aunt.

"When I left Helena's home, having just confessed

my deepest thoughts and feelings about a certain hellcat, I was surprised to come across a very familiar equine face in the stables."

She smiled, knowing that he had seen her horse. "But if you knew I was at your aunt's, why come here?"

He gave her hips a gentle squeeze so that she settled more comfortably on his lap. "If I confronted you at my aunt's house, you might have felt obliged to agree to whatever I asked, being put on the spot like that. But if you chose to come find me, to put yourself in my path again, I would know you wanted me. It's why I sent a letter to Helena telling her I planned to search for you in Penzance. I knew she would tell you. If you hadn't come, I would know that you wanted to continue to live your life all on your own. And if you did..."

He left the sentence unfinished, because they both knew what this meant for them. He tucked the carving into one of her hands, and she closed her fingers around it protectively. She'd made that figurine of his face so that she could always carry him with her.

"And if I did come after you, it was because I needed you in my life," she finished softly as she gazed deep into those whiskey brown eyes that always held her captive. "I already had you in my heart."

His eyes softened in a way that made her skin break out in goosebumps and he cuddled her closer against him.

"I'm afraid the man you know, the commanding man who has far too many opinions, probably half of them you disagree with is the man I truly am. Can you bear to live with that...with *me*?"

She smiled at him. "I don't imagine anyone but a hellcat like me could stand to, so I supposed I'd better," she teased. "It's a good thing I'm madly in love with you, even when you are being unreasonable and—"

He pressed a finger to her lips, silencing her, "I think you're saying things so that I'll bend you over my knee again."

Bridget giggled. "Perhaps I am...but I do love you."

"Madly?" he asked, his lips twitching.

"The maddest," she agreed.

"Good, then we'll be mad with love together." Trystan played with the length of ribbon at her chin. "I assume Marvella is waiting for you somewhere?" The restlessness that she'd always been so aware of seemed to be gone. He looked as if he could have sat there with her in his lap for the rest of his life.

"In my coach," Bridget said.

She stared at his face, taking in the sight of him. She had missed the way his whiskey-brown eyes enveloped her with their warmth, and the way it felt to have his large, elegant hands hold her. They'd had so little time like this, and this sweet intimacy between them was still so new. She even missed the way that he commanded her about and drove her to frustration with his silly lessons. Looking back all those moments now, she realized she'd started to fall in love with him that first day.

"I heard what you told lady Helena, all of it," she said after a moment.

His eyes warmed even more. "I felt a fool telling her all of that, but afterwards, I felt free. I didn't know you were there in the room listening."

"I'm sorry. I was in the back, in the sitting area. We had been talking when she heard you arrived, and she told me to hide."

Trystan smiled. "Cunning woman. I'd almost guess that she planned something of that sort."

"She is very clever," Bridget agreed.

He met her gaze. "So what are we to do, my little hellcat? Shall I court you like a proper lady? Then, on a fine spring day, I'll get down on one knee and ask you to marry me?"

She brushed her fingers over the back of his neck, lightly grazing her nails over him in the way she knew he liked.

"Perhaps you should just carry me off to the altar *now* before I fly away again."

"And create an even bigger scandal?" he asked. Worry colored his tone a little.

"Who cares about such trivial things?" she replied in all seriousness. "Kent and Graham wouldn't give me the cut direct and never speak to me again, would they?" Bridget queried, quite confident she knew what he'd say.

"Of course they wouldn't," Trystan replied without hesitation.

"Then your other friends won't either," she assured him.

He gazed at her, those warm brown eyes still worried. "You would risk it to be a countess?"

She lowered her head to his and kissed him, knowing they were in the middle of a grimy tavern and not caring at all.

"I don't *care* about being a countess. I only care about being with *you*." She nibbled his bottom lip, which made him groan softly.

"We had best leave before *I'm* the one who creates a scandal." He tossed a few coins on the table before he slid her off his lap and led her out of the tavern.

"We'll let Marvella follow us in your coach. You and I will take mine so we can talk."

She followed him as they explained matters to the two coach drivers and Marvella, then opened the door to his coach for her. He offered her his hand to climb inside.

"My lady fair..." he teased.

"Am I a fair lady?" she asked with a laugh.

"The fairest. Because I taught you to be."

"Oh hush, fancy pants," she shot back saucily. "I rather think I taught *you* a thing or two."

"You'll pay for that, hellion," he warned with a wicked gleam in his eyes.

"I certainly hope so." She raised her chin and purposely swayed her bottom in invitation before she sat on the coach seat.

Trystan climbed in after her and closed the door. He settled her back onto his lap, holding her close, then tugged on her bonnet ribbon again.

"You look quite delectable," he said. "I could nibble on you for days."

Bridget beamed at him. "I've had a number of new gowns made for me, and a bathing costume." She unfastened the ribbons of her bonnet and tossed it on the opposite bench.

"Tell me about all of your adventures. I want to hear everything."

"Everything?"

"Especially about you swimming at the beach."

She chuckled. "It could take a few days to tell all of it."

"Lucky for us we have the rest of our lives." Trystan's gaze softened, and she wanted to melt into him, to never be apart from him again.

"We do, don't we?" she said with a smug little grin.

"In that case, I have *other* things I'd like to do first." She toyed with his cravat and wriggled on his lap.

The wolfish look in his eyes returned. He fisted his hand in her hair and kissed her roughly, just the way she liked. Part of what attracted her to Trystan was that he never treated her as if she as if she might break during their moments of mutual passion. She kissed him back just as fiercely and soon they both pulled apart, needing to catch their breath.

He cupped her face in his hands and grinned. "I'm going to make love to you."

"Here?"

"Oh yes. Lift your skirts, my hellion." She quickly shimmied her gown up to her hips and he helped her straddle him, then freed himself from his trousers. He positioned her above him and then gripped her hips and pulled her down hard and fast onto him.

She gasped in surprise as she impaled herself on him. "Oh Trys!" This felt far different than the last time he'd made love to her. She felt full in a completely different way.

"That's it, little cat, ride me..." He groaned, rolling his hips up against her own.

Her earl was the most wicked man she'd ever known, and she wouldn't have him any other way. They were fully clothed and yet she was sliding up and down his shaft, their bodies moving as if they were one being. She clung to him, wrapping her arms around his neck as she met his lips in a fiery kiss that claimed her heart, body, and soul.

She came apart with a cry minutes later and collapsed on top of him. He held her close, stroking her hair and kissing the top of her head.

"That was simply glorious," she murmured drowsily against him. "*And* scandalous."

"That's only the *beginning*, hellcat." His dark promise of more passion made her smile.

"I knew the day I first saw you that you were dangerous," Bridget said.

"Dangerous?" he echoed, intrigued.

"Yes, dangerous."

"I rather think *you* were the dangerous one all along. Dangerous to my heart, little hellcat."

🕸️

THREE WEEKS LATER...

The remnants of the lavish wedding breakfast had been cleared away from the dining room, and all the wedding guests had retired to their private rooms in Trystan's massive house to rest before dinner.

Deep in the library, Bridget sat on a chaise, bathed in sunlight, holding a book and reading. Trystan's head lay in her lap as he stretched out on the couch, his eyes closed as he dozed. Her fingers drifted lazily through the silk strands of his hair. Earlier that morning, she'd said her marriage vows to him in the small local parish, and then stepped out into the sunlight, her hand upon his arm while their friends tossed rice and coins as they headed for their open carriage. The village children had scampered about, collecting the glittering coins on the ground. Everyone had cheered them on. A crowd of men and women from the highest echelons of society had attended the wedding, but all were trusted friends of Trystan.

Bridget knew at some point her past would likely come out, but she didn't care. By the time they were wed, the entire town of Zennor knew she was nothing more than a common bar wench, their words of course, but after a while the gossip settled down. After all, the villagers said, Trystan was half Romani, and wasn't it simply expected that he would do something rather risqué?

Bridget took it all in stride because she had Trystan and his friends fully supporting her. She didn't care that certain doors would remain closed to her or that some invitations would never come. No, what she cared about was spending time with Trystan and her growing circle of female friends who didn't care where she came from. Her adventures with Trystan were far from over and none of those adventures took place in ballrooms.

Lady Helena was right. She had herself. She had proven she could change her circumstances and her situation. She wouldn't let a few busybodies and gossips wreck her happiness. All that mattered was what she thought of herself. That was where her strength came from.

"You know..." Trystan spoke suddenly. Bridget closed her book and looked down at him.

"Hmm?"

"I'd completely forgotten this, but last year a band of Romani stayed on my land for a few weeks. Nothing unusual, I've done it before. The old mother of their tribe told me that I would someday find the woman meant for me."

"I'm sure she'd say that to anyone who was kind enough to let them stay."

"Perhaps. But she'd said I'd run from you, and I did... It was a miracle you loved my foolish heart enough to come after me. You are everything I could ever hope to love." He chuckled softly. "I used to think that molding you from clay would be the best way to create the perfect woman. But you proved me wrong. You have your own mind, your own heart, and those are what I cherish about you."

Bridget stared at her husband, then at the book of Greek mythology she had been reading. She stroked a fingertip along Trystan's straight nose, down to his sensual mouth. He kissed her fingertips and she smiled.

"I've been thinking about Graham," she said.

Her husband sat up abruptly. "Nothing bad, I hope."

She giggled and cuddled up against him, resting her chin on his shoulder as she looked at him.

"No, I was thinking of making a wager with you regarding him."

Trystan relaxed and kissed the top of her nose. "You have my attention. What are you thinking?"

"While I was staying in London with Marvella, I got to know the loveliest woman in London. She works in a flower shop. I think he would suit her well as a husband and she would make an excellent wife. They're quite the opposite in nature, but as we've rather discovered, opposites can be quite attractive. I wager I can trick him into marrying her."

Her husband released a booming laugh.

"Now that would be fun. What are the stakes?"

"If I fail to trick him into marriage, you win, and I'll let you..." She leaned in and whispered something terribly wicked in his ear. His eyes widened.

"You would be willing to try that?" he asked, shooting her a playful, leering look.

"Oh yes. But if I win..." She tapped her chin thoughtfully.

"If you win..." He smiled. "I'll do whatever you wish,

wife, because anything will be a dream as long as I'm with you... starting with that visit to Paris you and Marvella were planning."

She pushed him back on the chaise and crawled onto his lap, straddling him.

"Perhaps we should discuss our terms *further*..." She began to undo his neckcloth at the same time he undid the laces on the back of her gown.

The book she'd been reading fell to the floor and opened to the Greek myth she'd just finished reading. *Pygmalion.*

◈❧◈

Mrs. Story paused by the closed library door and grinned as she heard the giggles and laughter from inside. A footman stood next to the door, his face a little red, completely aware of what his master and mistress were up to.

"Make sure they aren't disturbed," she told him.

"Yes, Mrs. Story," he nodded.

Satisfied the lad would keep watch, she returned to her duties of cleaning up after the wedding breakfast. The home was still full of guests, and they had quite a lot to do to prepare for dinner that evening.

One of those guests came down the stairs as she

passed by. He was dressed in riding clothes and tugged on a pair of black riding gloves.

She greeted the handsome gentleman. "Good afternoon, Mr. Lennox."

"Good afternoon, Mrs. Story. Could you have someone bring my horse round?" he asked.

"Yes, of course, but take care riding if'n ye go too far. There is a wicked highwayman who's been robbing coaches and riders this past week."

Mr. Lennox's eyes widened. "A wicked highwayman? You don't say..."

"Oh yes, they say he's a charming one, but that doesna mean he isna dangerous."

"Thank you for the warning, Mrs. Story," Mr. Lennox said with a most curious smile.

A few minutes later, she passed by the front windows again and saw Mr. Lennox mount his horse. As he rode off, his great cloak unfurled behind him.

THANK YOU SO MUCH FOR READING THE EARL OF Zennor! The next book in the series will be _Her Wicked Highwayman_ which is all about our darling rogue Rafe Lennox! To find out when it releases follow me in one or more of these ways:

Sign up for my newsletter (be sure to add Lauren@

Laurensmithbooks.com to your contacts in your email address book so the newsletters don't go to spam)

Follow me on Book Bub HERE:https://www.book bub.com/authors/lauren-smith

Join my Facebook VIP Reader Group HERE:https://www.facebook.com/groups/400377546765661

Or become a patron on Patreon at either the **ebook** level where you get every new ebook release during the months you are an active subscriber, or be a **ebook and print** subscriber where you get **both** an ebook and a signed print book when they release while you are an active member. Learn more HERE:https://www.patreon.com/LSandECBooks

Made in United States
North Haven, CT
09 June 2023

37546993R00126